Cold As Ice

A Kellerman Mystery

By

Al Lamanda

Copyright 2016 by Al Lamanda

Other Kellerman Mystery Novels

Checkmate

Lollypops

Hard Time

Chapter One

Johnny Sanchez, the Alpha Male and Godfather of the Manhattan neighborhood known as Hell's Kitchen sat in a hardback chair and quietly sipped coffee from a deli container.

He's sixty-three-years-old, lean and fit and wore a pencil thin mustache that always reminded me of Clark Gable. He wore only suits custom made and the finest shirts and ties. His shoes were always imported Italian in the thousand dollar a pair range.

We were inside a warehouse he owned on Eleventh Avenue. The warehouse was full of furniture, boxes of DVD players, computers and flat screen TV sets. Two imported cars were parked against the back wall. A staircase led to a second floor office.

I've never asked Johnny about the warehouse or its contents. It's none of my business. All I know it that he has at least two additional warehouses on the West Side of the city.

Why is his business, not mine.

I stood behind Johnny and put my deli container of coffee beside a hard-wired phone on a table that served as a small desk. I opened my suit jacked and reached inside for my cigarettes and lit one with a paper match.

There was no point to asking Johnny how long we would have to wait for the cops to show up. He didn't know and he wouldn't tell me if he did. He was a patient man, perhaps the most patient man I've ever known.

And the most dangerous. I think those two characteristics, as far as Johnny is concerned are one and the same.

I picked up my coffee, sipped and smoked and waited.

The phone on the table rang. Johnny turned and picked it up. He listened for a moment, said, "Come ahead" and then hung up.

He looked over his shoulder and nodded to me. I put the cigarette out in an ashtray on the table and walked to the sliding metal door and pushed the 'up' button on the wall.

The door rose and a black Lincoln drove in and I hit the button marked 'down' and walked past the Lincoln and stood beside Johnny.

The front doors on the Lincoln opened and two city detectives got out. I didn't know who they were and had no desire to.

"The merchandise is in the trunk," one of the detectives said.

The two detectives went around to the trunk. It popped open and they removed two men from inside and tossed them to the cement floor.

"Okay, Johnny," one of the detectives said. "We owe you one."

"My pleasure, Lieutenant," Johnny said.

Both detectives returned to the Lincoln. I walked back to the button, opened the door and the Lincoln backed out and drove away. It had started to drizzle and the dark streets took on that reflective glow the way they always do when it rains.

I closed the door and looked at the two men on the floor. They were bound and gagged and had hoods over their heads.

I looked at Johnny. He nodded and I pulled out my pocket knife and cut their hands and legs free.

I stood behind them as they removed the hoods from their heads.

"Where are we?" one of them asked.

"Please don't ask questions," Johnny said.

"Who the fuck are you?" the other man said.

"I told you no questions," Johnny said.

"Hey, fuck you pop," the first man said.

I cleared my throat.

He turned and looked at me. "This goon don't frighten me," he said.

"Look at me," Johnny said. "Both of you."

They looked at Johnny.

"Your days of raping women are over," Johnny said.

"We were found not guilty," one of them said.

"The arresting officer forgot in his anxiousness to read you your rights," Johnny said. "Getting off on a technicality is not the same as being innocent."

"Fuck you, we're leaving," one of them said.

I stepped forward and punched him in the kidney and he fell to his knees.

"No, you're not," Johnny said. "You see, some in the police department still believe in justice. Due to a technicality in the law, you two miserable low-life's are walking the streets free while many of your victims are suffering in hospitals and mental institutions. So I am doing them a favor."

Johnny paused to pick up a pair of garden shears beside the phone. He held it in his hand and snipped the shears a few times. "Martha Stewart makes the best stuff, wouldn't you agree?"

"Hey, what is this," the man still standing said. "We got rights you know."

"So did your victims," Johnny said.

Johnny looked at me. I stepped forward and punched the second man in the kidney and he fell beside the first one. A hard kidney punch is devastating and difficult to recover from. That's why it's outlawed in boxing.

Johnny stood up with the garden shears. "Put them out," he told me.

The first man tried to stand and I put him down a right hook to the jaw. The second man was still on his knees and I kicked him in the face.

"Open their zippers," Johnny said.

"There's going to be a lot of blood," I said.

"As long as it isn't ours," Johnny said and went to work with the shears.

*****

I didn't ask about the private ambulance that just showed up afterward to take the two men to a hospital. Johnny wouldn't have told me anyway.

He drove us from the warehouse to the Bar and Grill on Ninth Avenue, an establishment he owns and uses as his headquarters.

Johnny drove a spotless white Cadillac in which I was never allowed to smoke and parked it in the municipal lot adjacent to the Bar and Grill. He didn't pay for parking as he owned the lot.

"Come in for a moment," Johnny said. "Some business I want to discuss."

Cindy was waiting tables, Saul, a sometimes substitute was behind the bar, the regular cook was in the kitchen, and the crowd was decent for a Wednesday night.

On the way to the office, Johnny stopped at the bar for a moment. "Saul, if you steal more than a hundred dollars tonight, I will have Kellerman beat you to a pulp."

"No problem," Saul said.

I've never asked Johnny why he allows Saul to steal from him on a regular basis. They go back fifty years or more and it's none of my business.

Johnny used a key to unlock his office door and we entered. Before the door even closed, Cindy handed me a large mug of coffee. I nodded and closed the door. Johnny went to the file cabinet beside his desk for the prized bottle of Black Maple Bourbon he always kept there and filled a water glass and took the chair behind his desk.

I took a chair opposite the desk and waited.

Johnny polished off half the glass of bourbon in one quick swallow. He looked at me and said, "Your woman has been home for two months and you haven't said two words about it."

"There's nothing to say," I said.

Johnny sighed, finished the glass of bourbon and quickly refilled it. "Your lawyer friend Cal Hawkins came to see me," he said.

"About Maria?" I said.

Johnny shook his head. "He wants to see you about another matter. Tomorrow night at seven-thirty."

I nodded.

"If you got a phone people wouldn't need to come to me to find you," Johnny said.

"True," I said. "But think of all the interesting people you wouldn't get to meet."

"What about Davis?" Johnny asked.

"I'm going to see him in the morning," I said. "Right now I'm going home and get some sleep."

"Thanks for your help tonight," Johnny said.

"No problem," I said.

Chapter Two

From my fourth floor bedroom window I had a clear line of sight to the Bar and Grill across the street. I own the building I live in. I picked it up a decade ago for ninety-seven-thousand-dollars at a city auction when the prior owner went bankrupt. I have no desire to be a landlord; I just needed a place to live and didn't want to pay rent. The building has sixteen apartments and one in the basement for a superintendent. Mrs. Parker, an eighty-year-old widow who lives on my floor is the building manager. I appointed her so the day I moved in. We made a deal. Tenants live rent free, but she collects a monthly fee from them to pay for building expenses and taxes. I don't know what the fee is and don't care. Everybody seems happy with the arrangement.

 I smoked a cigarette as I looked out the window. The rain was a fine mist now and the colors of the city reflected in puddles. Red and green from stoplights, neon from closed storefronts, the occasional yellow from a passing cab.

 I finished the cigarette and went to the bed where my cats were sleeping entwined around each other. Neither moved when I got under the covers. They were lazy creatures, but did their job of keeping mice away.

I thought about Maria for a while, hoping to get sleepy.

Maria Lopez, a drop dead gorgeous Puerto Rican, also was a Jersey cop for a dozen years. Her department was corrupt and indicted in a money laundering scheme and although she was clean, she received eighteen months for knowing and failing to report.

She served the full eighteen and was released two months ago. I picked her up at the prison she was sentenced to in West Virginia and we flew to New York in first class. She said not two words the entire flight.

At the airport, I rented a car and drove her to her small house in the suburbs. While she was incarcerated, I paid off the mortgagee and maintained the place for her. Except for the lack of flowers in the garden, things were pretty much the same.

I expected her to invite me in, but she didn't.

"Look, Kellerman, I'm grateful to you beyond belief for what you've done for me, but right now I need some time to be alone and think," she had said.

"I understand," I said, even though I didn't.

And still don't. I know prison, even a cushy women's facility where they play tennis everyday and watch cable TV at night can be hard and require some adjustment upon release, but I wasn't prepared to be cut off like a string hanging off a shirt.

I called her once a week and our conversations were always polite but cold. She wasn't ready to see me yet.

I fell asleep wondering and woke up with the cats pulling on my hair. I put on some coffee, fed the cats and changed their water, then took a shower. I smoked a cigarette at the window while I drank two cups of coffee, then changed into sweatpants and a grey tee-shirt.

The August sun was hot, even for seven-thirty in the morning while I jogged around pedestrians hurrying to work. My destination was the Y on 63rd Street near Central Park, about three quarters of a mile from my building.

I tossed weights around in the weight room for an hour, and then ran one hundred laps on the indoor track.

I was back in the apartment by nine forty-five and took a second shower. The cats were at the kitchen window, bird watching. Heavy iron gates on the windows prevent the cats from doing something stupid.

I wore a lightweight tan suit with a grey tee-shirt and black loafers when I left the apartment. My car was parked in Johnny's lot across the street. I tipped the guard at the gatehouse ten dollars for handing me the keys.

A few months ago, my thirty-year-old Olds finally up and died on me. I looked around and found a twenty-year-old Lincoln Continental with less than a hundred thousand miles on the engine and paid six grand for it. It was a comfortable ride with eight cylinders under the hood, but it wasn't the Olds.

I spent and hour fighting with traffic to reach the GW Bridge and then took the highway north for another to the state corrections facility for men where Davis was serving eighteen months on various charges.

I parked in the visitor's lot and went through the routine of gaining entrance, including a frisking and wand pat down before being escorted to the visitor's room.

Twelve chairs on each side of a thick glass. Each side had a phone. I took a vacant chair and waited. After a few minutes, a guard brought Davis to his chair.

We've been friends for twenty-five years. We met in the Marine Corps and served two tours in Iraq and Afghanistan. Afterward, we hooked up again in New York and formed an unbreakable bond of friendship. Or so I thought.

Davis, tall, black, a superior athlete also happens to be gay, something that never really mattered between us. Until he met and fell madly in love with a Broadway choreographer named Albert Kent.

Albert was heavy into drugs and before either of us knew it, Davis was a junkie. Things spiraled downward after that and Albert overdosed but Davis blames me for it and tried to kill me and Johnny one night at the Bar and Grill.

Johnny shot him.

Davis received two years, eligible for parole in eighteen.

I picked up the phone as did Davis.

"You don't look so good," I said. "Soft around the middle."

"It this bullshit orange uniform they make us wear," Davis said. "We all look like a fucking orange crop in here."

"I can have Cal Hawkins take your case for review," I said.

"Seeing as how I only going to kill you when I get out, why you want an early release for me?" Davis said.

"Because I still believe we're friends," I said. "Because I think deep down you know I'm right and that Albert was wrong for you."

"You believe wrong," Davis said.

"He made you a junkie," I said.

"I loved Albert and you had no right to kill him," Davis said. "And you gonna pay. Oh how you gonna fucking pay."

I hung up the phone.

Davis tapped on the glass.

I picked up the phone.

"Your woman out yet?" he asked.

"Two months now."

"Tell her hi for me."

"I would if she would see me."

"It like that, huh," Davis said.

"Like what?"

"In prison, she was turned," Davis said. "She come over to my side."

Grinning, Davis hung up.

*****

I grabbed lunch at a highway rest stop and then spent the afternoon at Roth's Gym on the West Side. At least eighty now, back in the day Roth was a contender for the lightweight title. He lost a split decision for the championship in 1960 and hung them up after the champion refused a rematch.

I jumped rope for thirty minutes, then worked the speed bag for thirty and ended with thirty minutes on a heavy bag.

Roth tracked me down in the locker room.

"Some lawyer was asking for you," he said. "He said he'd try the Pub."

"He found me," I said.

"Why don't you get a phone like the rest of the world?" Roth asked.

"If the rest of the world got smallpox, I should get it too?" I said.

"I don't even know what that means," Roth muttered and walked away.

*****

I arrived at The Bar and Grill around six and had a massive plate of roast beef with mashed potatoes and gravy. I washed it all down with iced water with lemon wedges. I read the sports pages while I ate.

My beloved Yankees were holding their own and were in second place in the eastern division. The Mets were in first place in their division, but I didn't really care.

Afterward, Cindy brought me coffee. Johnny emerged from his office and joined me in the booth. Cindy brought him bourbon over ice and when I fired up a cigarette, Johnny didn't blink at the violation of city law. Johnny has his own set of laws. If you want to smoke, smoke. If you don't like it, don't come in.

"Did you see Davis today?" Johnny asked.

"I did."

"And?"

"He says he's going to kill me when he gets out."

"That again," Johnny said. "Hell, I'm the one that shot him."

"Yeah but he still blames me for Albert's death," I said.

Johnny shrugged and sipped his drink.

"Something else he said," I said. "He said that the reason Maria doesn't want to see me that she was turned in prison."

"Went in straight and came out gay?"

I nodded.

"It's possible."

"I know," I said.

"Maybe you should find out?"

I looked past Johnny at Cal Hawkins as he entered the bar. He was pushing sixty, round in shape and wearing an expensive suit and toting a briefcase.

Johnny led the way to his office. He let Hawkins have the desk while I took a chair. Johnny stood at his file cabinet for easy access to his bourbon.

"This is a paying job, Kellerman," Hawkins said as he opened the briefcase.

Cindy knocked, opened the door and ushered in two mugs of coffee. She set the tray on the desk and left without saying a word.

"How much and what's the job?" I asked as I reached for a mug.

"Fifty thousand up front, fifty upon completion and expenses," Hawkins said.

"I don't do charity work," I said.

Hawkins glared at me. "You owe me for keeping Maria from a fifteen year stretch," he said. "Besides, the client's father used to be a member of the Bar and a man I once knew. I'd consider it a favor."

"Have a file?" I asked.

Hawkins produced a file from the briefcase and set it on the desk. "Read it. We'll have lunch tomorrow on me. It's not like you have anything better to do right now, right?"

"I'll read it tonight," I said. "Provided you look into an early release plea bargain for Davis."

"The man wants to kill you," Hawkins said.

"Just do it, okay."

"I'll make some calls."

"Thank you."

After Hawkins left, Johnny took his seat behind the desk.

"He has a point, the man wants to kill you," Johnny said.

I stood and picked up the file. "See you tomorrow," I said.

*****

Ellen Ashley Olsen was the client and she had quite the history. Born thirty-four years ago on Staten Island, her mother was a school teacher, he father an estate lawyer. She was a normal kid in an upper middle class neighborhood until after graduating high school, she met Brian Cosby.

Cosby was four years older, a handsome kid by all accounts and a heavy drug user. He was well known to the cops as a pusher, having several arrests on his sheet and try as they might, her parents weren't able to keep Ellen away from him.

They ran away together when Ellen was just nineteen.

Cosby also came from money, but his parents cut him off when he refused to get clean. That's when, as the junkies used to refer to it, they traveled the circuit. Constantly on the move from state to state, scoring drugs, committing robberies to pay for their freight, staying one step ahead of the cops.

Sometimes, when broke enough, Ellen would walk the streets and Cosby would roll the Johns.

Ten years ago, Ellen became pregnant. The father could be Cosby or a John. It didn't really matter. Since they never married, Cosby devised that as an unwed mother, Ellen might qualify for welfare. They returned to Staten Island and she applied for and received benefits. They also tried to hit up her parents for money and to a degree, it worked.

Cosby continued to sell and pimp Ellen almost to the time she gave birth to an addicted baby boy.

Needless to say, child services were immediately notified by the hospital and the child, upon rehabilitation was placed into his grandparent's care with one stipulation. Ellen would have no contact with her son.

Ellen was arrested and tried for child endangerment and a Staten Island judge gave her the maximum of seven years.

A warrant for Cosby's arrest failed to produce him and to this day he's still at large.

Six months after the baby came to live with Ellen's parents, while her father was at work, someone broke into their home, killed her mother and stole the baby. Hawkins used the word stole rather than kidnapped because ransom demands were never forthcoming.

Everybody suspected Cosby, but nobody could find or prove his involvement. After a while, years in fact, police and the FBI put the case on the back burner. Time passed and everybody moved on.

After his wife died, Ellen's father never really returned to work and he sold his practice. Money wasn't a factor, he had plenty, but his spirits were broken and he rarely left the house except to visit Ellen on occasion at the prison in upstate New York.

Three years ago, after serving every day of her seven year stretch, Ellen was released. She was healthy, having kicked the drug habit under prison doctor care and took many college courses using the library computers. Her father picked her up and took her in and she got a job at a small accounting firm as an office manager.

Ellen pressed the police and FBI about her baby, but their lack of progress all but closed the case.

Life went on and three months ago, Ellen's father passed away after suffering a heart attack.

Simply put, Ellen wants to know what happened to her son.

I was on my bed with the cats sleeping at my feet. I reached over to the nightstand for my cigarettes.

I lit one and blew smoke.

"Good luck with that," I said as I closed the file.

Chapter Three

In the morning, I walked across the hall and knocked on Mrs. Parker's apartment door. After a few seconds, the lock turned and the door opened as far as the chain would allow it.

"I need your phone," I said.

She nodded, left for a moment and returned with a cordless phone.

"I'm about to make breakfast," she said. "Would you care to join me?"

"Give me ten minutes," I said.

She closed the door and I sat on the hallway steps.

I tried Hawkins at home and he hadn't left for his office yet.

"Do I look like Saint Jude to you?" I said when he answered the phone.

"Who?"

"The Patron Saint of Lost Causes."

"I take it you read the file?"

"I read it," I said. "My answer is no, it's not doable."

"Take the case, take the money and I'll do Davis pro bono," Hawkins said. "Besides, everything isn't in the file."

"Like what?"

"Like be at my office at eleven and find out," Hawkins said and hung up.

"Shit," I said.

I stood and knocked on Mrs. Parker's door. She opened it and I entered her apartment.

"Kitchen," she said.

Mrs. Parker made French toast with sides of bacon and sausage and toast, orange juice and coffee.

We chatted about the building as we ate. What needed paint and repair, a new tenant, the superintendent wanted to buy a dozen new garbage cans, tenant complaints and the upcoming taxes.

We met like this once a month.

I usually told her to just handle it.

"If you don't mind me saying so, you seem distracted today," Mrs. Parker said when business was concluded.

"It's nothing," I said. "I have to go. I have to make a meeting."

Mrs. Parker never asked my business. She just accepted things as they were.

*****

I wore a light grey suit with a matching tee-shirt and black loafers to Hawkins's Park Avenue South office.

The lavish building stood forty floors high. Hawkins's office was on twenty and faced the street.

His secretary ushered me to his back office. "Would you café for coffee?" she asked before she closed the door behind her.

"I would."

"Sit," Hawkins said.

I sat.

"The police and FBI couldn't find the …" I said.

There was a knock on the door. It opened and the secretary walked in and handed me a mug of coffee.

"Hold any calls," Hawkins said.

She nodded and closed the door.

"I know all about the police and FBI," Hawkins said. "Ralph Olsen and his wife Judith were friends of mine. Ralph had an office on eighteen in this very building. No one should have the heartache those two endured."

"The kid is gone, Cal, and he's not coming back," I said.

"I told Ellen we would be by her house around one-thirty," Hawkins said. "We'll talk more on the way."

*****

"I will file a motion to have his sentence reduced to one year," Hawkins said. "Davis will be out in nine."

I nodded.

"Seeing as how he wants to kill you, I don't understand why you want him released at all," Hawkins said.

"He's my friend."

"Was," Hawkins said. "Was your friend."

"I don't throw away my friends like a worn shirt just because they're having some problems," I said.

"Okay," Hawkins said.

He drove to the ferry and we sailed across to Staten Island with neither of us leaving his car.

On the other side, he drove for about thirty minutes to an upper-middle-class neighborhood near the shore.

He parked in the driveway in front of an open garage where a blue Ford Bronco took up one of three spaces.

I put the home in the seven hundred thousand dollar range.

The woman who answered the door was nothing like what I expected. Ellen Ashley Olson was all of five-feet-one inches tall, with long blond hair and piercing blue eyes.

She seemed, for someone with her past to be very healthy.

"Mr. Hawkins," she said when she opened the door.

"This is Kellerman, the man I told you about," Hawkins said.

"Hello," Ellen said. "Please come in."

*****

Ellen poured coffee from a glass carafe. She wore a teal tank top with blue jeans and as she filled three cups, I checked her arms for track marks. She sat and smiled at me.

"Between my toes and the back of my knees," she said to me. "That's what you're looking for, isn't it? Track marks."

"I was noticing how healthy and toned you look," I said.

"For a junkie you mean?" Ellen said.

"I didn't say that," I said.

"But you were thinking it?"

"Yes."

"I've been clean for nine years," Ellen said. "The best thing that ever happened to me was going to prison. I got a degree in accounting and manage a small firm here on the Island. The last three years with my dad were the best years I've ever had with him. I eat right and exercise regularly. My last checkup with my doctor gave me a clean bill of health. The worst thing in my life was losing my son and mother's murder. The second worst thing in my life was meeting Brian Cosby who caused the first."

I nodded. "Mind if I smoke?"

"Go ahead," Ellen said as she stood and opened a cabinet for an ash tray.

"I have to be honest with you," I said. "I feel you don't deserve to be reunited with your son if he is alive that is."

"I have every reason to believe he is alive," Ellen said. "The FBI never reported to me that they believe otherwise. They believe it was Brian that murdered my mother and kidnapped my son. You see Mr. Kellerman, this is a big demand for black market babies and Brian probably sold the baby for the money. At least that's what the FBI believed at the time."

"I'm well aware of the black market for babies," I said as I lit a cigarette. "And my feeling hasn't changed. The baby is better off not knowing who his mother is. He's ten now and probably a happy, well-adjusted kid. Why screw with that?"

Ellen looked at Hawkins. "You didn't tell him?"

"Tell me what?" I asked.

"I don't want to be reunited with my son," Ellen said. "I agree with you that he is better off where he is. You see, my father left me this house and two hundred and fifty thousand in cash. He also left four hundred thousand to my son in trust if and when he can be found. His will is quite specific. I helped him write it. My son is to be given the money without knowing where it came from. He is as you said, probably happy, but who couldn't use that kind of money to jumpstart your life. If you can locate him, you give him the trust fund that he can't use until he is eighteen and ready for college."

I blew smoke and looked at Hawkins. He shrugged at me.

"What makes you think I can do what the FBI couldn't?" I asked Ellen.

"I've known Mr. Hawkins all my life," Ellen said. "He says you can get things done while others can't. I believe him."

I sat back for a moment and thought. I really didn't have much else to do these days except sit around and moon over Maria and try to salvage my friendship with Davis.

"Give me twenty-four hours to think it over," I said. "Have ready any photos you might have of Brian and a list of names of past friends, hangouts and places he might be hiding in if he's even still alive."

Ellen nodded. "If you return at ten, that's only eighteen hours to think it over," she said.

I looked at her.

She smiled.

"Then make it two o'clock and have lunch ready," I said. "I think better while I eat."

"What kind of food do you like?" Ellen asked.

"Whatever is bad for me," I said.

*****

"You conniving little prick," I said to Hawkins as the ferry took us back to Manhattan.

"Like you have anything better to do at the moment," Hawkins said. "Besides, if you're successful you just might change the boy's life for the better and pick up a hundred grand to boot."

"And you get what?"

"The satisfaction of helping an old friend and nothing more, you miserable bastard," Hawkins said.

"No," I said. "What you get to do is pro bono work for Davis. If you backtrack on that I'll throw you out your office fucking window."

"So we have an accord?" Hawkins said.

"Yeah, we have an accord," I said.

Chapter Four

I played chess with Johnny until nine in the evening. We played a marathon game of eighty-nine moves before we called the game a draw.

During the game I drank and entire pot of coffee and Johnny consumed a fifth of bourbon. His capacity for alcohol is second to none. If he's ever drunk, it never shows.

Game over, Johnny finally asked, "Your lawyer friend, are you going to agree?"

The game lasted four plus house and he waited until we were finished to ask his question. He could outwait any man I knew.

"Haven't decided yet."

"It seems like an easy six figures to me."

"Nothing is ever easy," I said. "And I'm far from broke."

"But you'll do it," Johnny said. "We both know that."

*****

After I left Johnny, I retrieved the Lincoln from the lot and drove south to the tunnel and crossed over to Jersey. I drove around for a bit until I mentally committed to staking out Maria's house.

I found a deli and picked up two large containers of coffee and then drove to the quiet, tree-lined street where Maria's house was the last one on the block. It was after eleven by the time I parked across the street a hundred feet away in front of an empty lot. Most of the houses were dark, a few with floodlights above the door.

Two lights were on in Maria's house, the kitchen and living room. The garage door was closed so I couldn't see if her car was parked inside.

I removed the lid from a container, lit a smoke, sipped and waited. By the time the first container was empty and three cigarettes were smoked, I was convinced Maria wasn't home. Nothing moved in the kitchen, no shadow crossed the light in either room; no other lights went on or off.

I started on the second container and smoked a few more cigarettes. I decided to call it a night after the second container was empty. I left the car and walked into the empty lot to piss out all the coffee.

I was just zipping up when car lights turned the corner and I spotted Maria's car. It quickly braked and pulled into her driveway. She remote accessed the garage door, it flipped up and she pulled in and the door closed.

I returned to the Lincoln and sat in the dark. I lit another cigarette and found my hands were a bit clammy.

I watched the house. With the shades down in the kitchen, I couldn't positively identify the figure I saw walk past the window as Maria, but it certainly looked like her.

The refrigerator door opened.

Then, at the same time a second figure appeared in the bedroom window behind the drawn curtains.

It was the outline of a woman. She removed her top and tossed it aside.

In the kitchen, the light went out and a few moments later, Maria entered the bedroom and the two figures embraced.

I started the engine, put the Lincoln in gear and speed away from the curb.

*****

In my apartment, I stood under a hot shower for thirty minutes. When I finally emerged, I tossed on a robe, grabbed a bottle of water from the fridge and went to bed.

The cats, asleep in the center, looked at me with indication when I turned down the sheets.

I smoked a few cigarettes and sipped water and thought about Maria.

Davis, the son of a bitch, apparently was right in his analysis.

She had, obviously entered into a relationship with a woman. I thought about my options and concluded there were none.

Although I paid off the mortgage on her house so she wouldn't lose it and paid off her car so she could keep it, she owed me nothing because she didn't ask me to do it.

I never asked her to marry me nor gave her a ring, so the lack of commitment on my part was my own fault.

I switched gears and thought about Ellen Ashley Olson. The odds of actually finding her son after a decade were nonexistent at best.

As Hawkins said, it was a quick hundred grand and something to do.

Chapter Five

I grabbed a light breakfast at the coffee shop on West 57th and skimmed the sports pages while I ate.

Then I walked over to the Y and did an hour in the weight room followed by a hundred laps on the track. I was back in my apartment, showered and dressed by ten in the morning.

On the way to the library, I picked up a large coffee and brought it in with me. It wasn't the main branch, far from it, but the computer room had eight computers and the librarians always let me use one for as long as I needed in exchange for a thousand dollar yearly donation.

After a librarian signed me into a terminal, I went to work.

A Google search of archived police reports on the murder of Clair Ellen Fallen brought up a lot. She was forty-nine-years-old at the time of her murder. She was on summer break from teaching school when, sometime after ten in the morning an intruder entered the home while she was in the shower.

Her naked body was found in the bedroom where the baby slept in a crib. The crib was empty when police arrived on the scene. Clair died hard. Her face was battered and bruised, blood was found under her fingernails and he knuckles were scraped and cut. She fought to her last breath to protect the baby before the intruder strangled her to death.

A neighbor walking their dog across the street noticed a man wearing a grey hooded sweatshirt with a wrapped bundle in his arms enter a dark car parked in front of the Fallen home and called 911.

James Fallon was in his Park Avenue South office at the time with a client. Ellen, his daughter, was serving her sentence in upstate New York and neither was a suspect in the brutal murder.

The police handled it as a murder.

The FBI dealt with it as a kidnapping.

Neither had any success in solving the murder or locating and returning the child even though all involved knew or suspected the murderer and kidnapper to be Brian Cosby.

I switched over to Ellen's father and by all accounts, he was a highly regarded estate attorney with many clients in the millionaire and celebrity bracket. He had a clean arrest and driving record right up to the day he died.

Clair was a middle school teacher with twenty-five years experience. The photo of her in the newspaper was black and white and grainy, but it was clear she was a handsome woman with blonde hair and bright eyes.

A search of Brian Cosby brought up his arrest record going back to his first at age fifteen to his last at age twenty-two. Everything from shoplifting, robbing drugstores, snatching purses, rolling drunks and possession of illegal substances. He seemingly fell off the earth after Clair's murder and the kidnapping of the baby.

I had no doubt that he killed Clair, stole the baby and sold it on the black market.

Junkies will do anything for a fix, including selling their own flesh and blood.

Ellen Ashley Fallen had a rap sheet of minor offenses. Mostly shoplifting and purse snatching and prostitution. Oddly enough she was never picked up for drugs.

I left the library and walked to the lot to retrieve the Lincoln.

*****

"Come in," Ellen said after I rang the bell and she answered the door.

She wore a teal colored tank top with tan shorts and white jogging shoes. Her hair was worn in a ponytail and he face was void of any traceable makeup.

"I picked up steaks," Ellen said. "You look like a steak kind of guy. The grill is in the backyard. We can talk while you cook."

I followed her to the kitchen where sliding glass doors led to the backyard. It was about a thousand square feet of neatly mowed lawn, several flowerbeds and bricked patio area with a stainless steel grill.

There was a pot of coffee, cups, a pitcher of lemonade and glasses and a platter with two steaks on it on the patio table.

"I like this look better," Ellen said.

"What look?"

"Jeans, pullover shirt, running shoes," Ellen said. "The suit you wore yesterday appeared too formal. Start the grill and let it heat up first."

I went to the grill and activated all three burners.

When I returned to the table, Ellen had filled two cups with coffee.

"Go ahead and smoke if you're inclined," she said.

I sat opposite her, lit a cigarette and sampled the coffee.

Ellen reached onto the vacant seat next to her and produced a yellow legal pad.

"I did as you asked," she said. "I made a list of all his friends as I knew them from before I went to prison. The few photos I do have are at least eight to ten years old."

I looked at the envelope on top of the legal pad.

Ellen opened the envelope and removed a handful of photos. Three were black and white wallet size photos taken at what looked like a state fair.

"Those are at least ten years old," she said. "The others I'm not sure. Things are kind of a blur back then."

Brian Cosby was a good looking, all American boy type. Sandy hair, nice smile, white even teeth, twinkling brown eyes, the kind you'd let mow your lawn, carry in your groceries and date your daughter.

"One thing," I said. "Keep in mind every question I ask has a purpose. Anything and everything can possibly mean and lead to something else. I ask, you answer. Those are the rules. Agreed?"

Ellen nodded.

"Let's start with how and when you first met Brian."

"Senior year of high school," Ellen said. "I was the wallflower of my class. I had braces from the age of sixteen when I developed an overbite. I was shy and felt awkward around boys. One afternoon during lunch period, I …"

"What high school?" I asked.

"Regional," Ellen said. "My parents had the money to send me to private school, but I insisted I go to Regional like everyone else in the neighborhood."

"So one afternoon what?" I asked.

"I was sitting on a bench on the school grounds," Ellen said. "It was April, I think. A small crowd of kids were buying pot from Brian and he must have spotted me because afterward, he came and joined me on the bench. He was so good looking with this charming smile; I couldn't believe he wanted to talk to me. Before the next class, he asked me on a date. I said yes. Keep in mind the number of dates I had the entire four years in high school I could count on one hand. The grill should be hot enough now."

I picked up the plate with the steaks, carried it to the grill and used tongs to place them on the fire.

"So how did the date go?" I said as I returned to the table.

"We saw a movie, had burgers afterward and he introduced me to pot in his car," Ellen said. "Don't let the talking heads fool you with their rhetoric about the harmless pleasure of pot, that's bullshit. I know. I drove that car down that road."

"And after that?"

"More dates, more pot," Ellen said. "A gradual upgrade to coke and then the final push to heroin. First chasing the dragon and then mainlining. Do you know what chasing the dragon is?"

"Yes."

"You don't do drugs?"

"No."

"Ever?"

"No."

"What's that you're smoking?"

"I'll give you that one," I said. "Go on."

"Better flip the steaks."

I flipped the steaks and returned to the table.

Ellen picked up my pack of cigarettes. "I used to love to smoke," she said. "I can't anymore. Know why?"

"Nicotine is a mental addiction and can be classified as a gateway substance to a recovering addict," I said.

"You're very smart."

"Continue," I said.

"I was hooked almost immediately," Ellen said. "At first, I hid it well, so I thought. Mom caught on before dad. That was right after graduation when I refused to go to college. Dad went to NYU and Columbia. I skipped out with Brian and we went on the road. That really opened my eyes."

"How so?"

"Brian had contacts everywhere," Ellen said. "From Jersey to Kansas City to Maine and Florida. We'd drive stoned and God only knew how we got where we were going. Brian would mail our junk to a friend so if we were stopped there was no drugs in the car except for the small amount we needed to keep straight. When we reached our destination, Brian would fetch our junk and he'd sell pot to kids to buy more junk. It was an endless cycle. We'd sell drugs to get the money to buy more drugs and use what we needed to get straight so we could sell more drugs to buy more drugs. By traveling a lot we stayed under the radar of the cops."

"This went on for how long?"

"About six years," Ellen said. "Toward the end it was pretty bad. We shoplifted from stores, mugged old ladies and I took to the streets. I still had some youthful looks and could get fifty for a quick lay or blowjob. Better check the steaks."

I checked the steaks. They were done and I put them on a clean plate and took them to the table. Ellen had returned to the kitchen and reappeared with a bowl of mashed potatoes and baked beans.

"I usually have just a salad for lunch, so this is a treat for me," Ellen said.

I sliced into my steak and forked a piece into my mouth. It was medium and tender.

"After that came the baby?" I said.

Ellen nodded. "It's a miracle pregnant is all I got," she said. "No HIV, no AIDS, no STD's, just pregnant. I have a nice chocolate cake for dessert by the way."

"Do you know for certain the baby is Cosby's?"

"No. It probably is, but I was turning a lot of tricks back then."

"The scheme was?"

"Simple and idiotic," Ellen said. "Although we thought we were so very clever at the time. Staten Island was still my home address. Brian figured as an unwed mother I could get welfare while putting the so-called arm on my parents. Neither of us in our clouded state of mind figured Social Services were as competent as they were. My son was born a junkie, I was arrested for child endangerment and Brian skipped town."

"Is there any doubt in your mind it was Cosby that murdered your mother and kidnapped the baby?"

"None. It's exactly the kind of thing he would do," Ellen said. "He's hurt others. I don't know if he killed anyone before, but I know he's beaten and knifed others."

"What about his parents?"

"Both disowned him before I met him," Ellen said. "All I know is they retired and moved to Florida."

"Did your father leave you anything else besides the house and cash?" I asked.

"Fifty thousand in gold. Fifty thousand in stock. A small cottage on a lake in New Hampshire. I haven't been there since I was seventeen."

"Has Cosby ever tried to contact you?"

"No. He very well could be dead for all I know."

"The list of names," I said.

"It's everyone I could think of," Ellen said. "If I remember any others I'll let you know."

"I have a license from the state as a private investigator, but it's mostly just an excuse to carry a gun inside the city," I said. "I work under the table and by that I mean I follow nobody's rules but my own. If you want an above board investigator who dots the I's and crosses the T's, I'm not your man. Do we understand each other?"

"Mr. Hawkins said you were the toughest son of a bitch around and a man who can get things done," Ellen said. "We understand each other."

"Good. Did you bake the cake yourself?"

*****

"So what now?" Ellen asked as she walked me to my car.

"Do you work tomorrow?"

"Eight to four-thirty," Ellen said.

"Can you meet me in the city around seven-thirty?"

"I can. Why?"

"Bring fifty thousand in the form of a cashier's check and twenty thousand in cash for expenses," I said. "I don't do receipts so consider the twenty thousand lost."

Ellen nodded. "Where?"

"Are you familiar with Manhattan?"

"Yes."

"The Bar and Grill on Ninth Avenue between Fifty-second and third."

"I'll be there," Ellen said.

I took the folder with me and drove back to the ferry. I smoked a cigarette in the car as the ferry crossed over to lower Manhattan. I was back in my apartment by six o'clock.

The cats were happy to see me and greeted me at the door, but that was mostly because their food bowl was empty.

I loaded up the bowl, changed the water in their dish and put on some coffee.

I sat at the table with a cup and opened the file. I scanned the list of names and counted twenty-seven. Some had states of residence, most had nothing. I looked at the photos of Brian Cosby. He had the conniving little smile of a con man.

I closed the file and went down the hall and knocked on Mrs. Parker's door.

"Mrs. Parker, I'd like to borrow your phone," I said.

The door opened and she handed me the phone.

"Thank you," I said.

I sat on the steps and dialed Maria's number. It rang four times and the answering machine picked up. I waited for the message to play through and then I said, "Maria, it's Kellerman. I wanted to …"

"I'm here," Maria said. "I screen calls these days."

"How are you?"

"Good. You?"

"I want to see you," I said.

"Not a good idea right now."

"How come?"

"It's just not," Maria said. "I'm starting a new job and I have a lot of things to work out in my mind. I can never be a cop again, you know. I'm still coming to grips with that."

"We can still talk," I said. "Maybe I can even help?"

There was a noise in the background and Maria said, "I'll call you soon," and hung up.

*****

I was parked across the street from Maria's house far enough away so that in the dark I couldn't be seen.

I had two containers of coffee and a lemon danish. I nibbled on the danish and sipped as I watched the house. She was home. Lights were on in every room and I could see her moving around from room to room.

The second container was empty and I was going to call it a night when a sports car turned the corner and pulled into Maria's driveway. A slinky brunette got out and walked to the door. She was carrying an overnight bag.

She used a key to let herself in.

I started the engine and headed for home.

Chapter Six

I skipped the Y and went right to Roth's Gym after a light breakfast at the coffee shop on West 57th.

After thirty minutes of skipping rope, I switched to the speed bag for another thirty and ended with one hour on the heavy bag. Drenched in sweat I took a chair next to Roth who was watching two heavyweights spar in the ring.

They were sloppy four rounders at best, hugging and leaning on each other, occasionally tossing a punch.

"These guys have the endurance of a newborn," I said.

"Boxing is in a sorry state of affairs," Roth said. He stood up and shook his fist. "Hey, are you goons gonna fight or fuck? If you wanna fuck, go get a room and get out of my ring."

I left Roth screaming and shaking his fist and walked home.

*****

I dropped a check for a thousand dollars with the library branch manager before finding a free computer terminal. A sign read *Thirty Minute Per Terminal*, but everybody knew I would ignore it.

I had Ellen's folder and opened it and went right to work on the list of names. Many were common first and last names, so I used arrest records to weed and narrow it down.

After about and hour, I left for coffee and a cigarette. Things were untouched when I returned.

By two in the afternoon, I crossed off fifteen of the twenty-eight names. There was no sense checking people that were dead. Finding twelve would be chore enough.

On the way home I picked up some Italian. My cats have developed a taste for pasta and sauce and I treated them to a bowl with a cut up meatball.

Afterward the three of us took a nap on the bed.

I slept until five. When I got up, the cats carried on without me. I shaved using the fairly new electric shaver I bought when I grew tired of buying blades at five bucks a pop.

After I shower, I dressed in a dark blue warm-up suit with jogging shoes.

*****

I killed some time over a game of chess with Johnny. We played until seven-fifteen and ended the game in a draw.

"When was the last time I actually won a game?" I asked.

"You know whenever you do win. It's because I always let you, don't you?" Johnny said.

"I suspected."

At seven twenty-five, the door opened and Ellen walked in. She wore stylish jeans with a designer top and boots. Her hair was down and a bit longer than I expected. She carried and oversize handbag that hung off her right shoulder.

"The client?" Johnny said.

Ellen spotted me and as she walked to the table, I stood.

"This is my associate John Sanchez," I said. "We'll be using his office."

Johnny stood and led the way into his office.

"Would you care for a drink, a glass of wine?" Johnny asked.

"I can't do alcohol," Ellen said.

"Of course," Johnny said. "A soft drink perhaps?"

"Coke with ice," Ellen said.

Johnny picked up his phone and asked for Coke with ice and coffee for me.

A minute later, Cindy arrived with a tray.

"Thank you," Ellen said as she took the Coke.

I sat behind the desk while Johnny went to the file cabinet, but didn't open it.

Ellen took a chair opposite the desk.

"I whittled down the list you gave me to twelve," I said. "Fifteen names are dead."

"That doesn't surprise me," Ellen said. "Junkies have a short life span."

"I'm going to start with the twelve and see where that goes," I said. "If I need you I know how to get in touch with you except for your cell number. Write that down. If you need to get in touch with me, call here and Johnny will get a hold of me."

"Don't you have a phone?" Ellen asked.

"No."

"Not even a cell?"

"Especially a cell."

Ellen sipped from her glass. "Part of your own rules?"

"Yes. Do you have the first payment and expense money?"

Ellen nodded.

"Give the check to Johnny and the expense money to me."

Ellen opened her oversize bag, reached in and produced two envelopes. One was thin, the other about an inch thick. She handed Johnny the thin envelope and set the thick one on the desk.

Johnny turned to the closet next to the file cabinet, opened the door and put the check into his open safe.

"I'm now working for you," I said. "But remember my rules. I run the show and you answer to me Anytime you want to call it quits just say the word. Are you pressed for time?"

"No."

"I'd like to talk a while," I said. "Would it bother you to sit at a booth in the bar?"

"No."

Johnny stayed in the office while Ellen and I went to the booth where Johnny and I played chess. The board was still in place.

"Who won?" Ellen asked.

"Draw."

"Do you play a lot?"

"Only with Johnny."

"I was on my high school chess team," Ellen said.

"Set up the board," I said. "We can talk and play at the same time. I'll get you a fresh Coke."

I went to the bar where Cindy had taken over for Johnny earlier and asked for a tall Coke with ice and a mug of coffee for me and took them back to the table.

Ellen had white because that side of the board faced her when we first sat down.

"Make your move and we'll talk as we play," I said.

Ellen nodded, looked at the board and moved her knight's pawn one space.

"Can you remember if Cosby has a favorite color?" I said as I moved my bishop's pawn one space.

"I don't know that it was his favorite, but he wore dark blue a lot," Ellen said.

She brought out a knight.

"Any particular kind of car he liked over others?"

"Not really. Older cars that wouldn't attract attention. Dark colors and mostly four doors," Ellen said. "He could steal an older car in nothing flat. Newer cars with all the stuff they put in them now are almost impossible to steal clean."

"Clean?" I said as I moved out a bishop.

"If you have to break a window to gain access it's not exactly drivable around town," Ellen said. "And newer cars are almost impossible to hotwire, or at least they were ten years ago when they first started putting in all the sensors and computer chips."

Ellen moved the pawn in front of a bishop.

"Was he violent?" I asked. "You said yesterday he hurt some people, but was he violent?"

"I don't … that doesn't make sense," Ellen said. "Isn't hurting people violent?"

"Not necessarily," I said. "Violence can be used as a tool to an end without the person using that tool being violent by nature."

Ellen looked at me. "Are you talking about yourself?"

"I am," I said. "So was Cosby nonviolent by nature and used violence when it was necessary, or was it is nature to be violent."

I moved my bishop across the board.

"Brian was a charmer and a schemer," Ellen said. "He got by on his looks, smile and wit. But when he needed a fix, he could get ugly. You could say that about all junkies, including myself."

"He ever hit you?" I asked.

"Not that I recall," Ellen said.

Ellen moved her second knight out.

"Was he into sports or have any hobbies?" I asked.

"Junkies have one sport, outrunning the cops and one hobby, getting high," Ellen said.

"I get that, but did he every talk sports or movies, things like that?"

"No sports I can remember," Ellen said. "He did like that movie about junkies, Drugstore Cowboy. I think he got a lot of ideas from that movie. Ever see it?"

"No."

I slid my bishop across the board and captured Ellen's first knight.

She studied the board.

"Before you went to prison, did you see Cosby at all?" I asked.

"The last time I saw him was at the hospital the night I gave birth," Ellen said. "He drove me there from the shitty one bedroom apartment we were staying in, left me at emergency and took off. I was arrested almost immediately after the baby was born. The doctors knew before I even went into delivery the baby would come out hooked and they notified the police and my parents. I'm grateful that the doctors knew what to do and my baby lived. I'm also grateful that the police and social services sent me to prison or I probably wouldn't be sitting here playing chess with you right now."

"It's your move," I said.

Ellen blocked my bishop with a pawn.

"The police go to the apartment?" I asked.

"They were too late," Ellen said. "He packed his stuff and was gone by the time they arrived. I was in labor for nine hours. A junkie can get seriously lost in nine hours."

"And he stayed lost for six months until he kidnapped the baby and murdered your mother?" I said.

"As far as I know," Ellen said. "Like I said, the police and FBI never found him. He might very well be dead for quite a while."

I moved my knight into attack position.

Ellen studied the board. "You play very well."

"If you had to pick one place where Cosby would go to and disappear, where would that be?" I asked.

Ellen sat back and thought for a moment. "I have no idea," she said. "Brian is a junkie and by definition that makes him a sneaky, lying bastard. When I think back on it, I don't think he was ever truthful with me once."

"Your move," I said.

Ellen brought out her pawn to counter my bishop.

"Tomorrow I start on the remaining twelve names," I said.

Ellen nodded. "I don't think I can beat you. My game is very rusty."

"I'm done for now anyway," I said.

Ellen glanced at the delicate watch on her left wrist. "I have just enough time to make the meeting at Saint Paul's," she said.

"AA?"

She nodded.

"Mind if I tag along?"

"I don't mind. Is this research?"

"In a sense."

We left the bar and I nodded to Cindy on the way out.

"We'll take my car," I said.

*****

"My name is Annemarie and I'm an alcoholic," the woman at the podium said.

We were in the basement meeting room of Saint Paul's. There were forty chairs assembled around the podium. Thirty were filled, not counting the chairs Ellen and I occupied. We each had a container of coffee from the table against the wall. I skipped the donuts, but Ellen happily grabbed a Boston cream.

We listened to Annemarie's sad tale of her downward spiral into the dark and lonely world of alcoholism. She received a warm round of applause when finished.

Almost everybody was smoking and I gratefully joined in.

Several more speakers told us their tales. One, a man, was a recovering heroin addict. He said there is nothing that compares to the pleasure of a heroin high except for sobriety.

After the meeting, we walked the deserted streets to my car parked two blocks from the church. Lower Manhattan at night is an empty, desolate place. Ellen took my right arm.

"That's quite the bicep you have Mr. Kellerman," she said.

"Drop the mister."

"I could see right off you spend a lot of time in a gym."

"I do," I said as I unlocked the car and opened the door for Ellen. Once she was in, I went around to the driver's side.

"You have very good manners for a thug," Ellen said as I started the engine.

"Who said I'm a thug?" I said as I pulled away from the curb.

"Mr. Hawkins," Ellen said. "He said you were a complete thug, very dangerous, but highly efficient and very smart."

"I'll take it as a compliment," I said. "What does it feel like being on heroin?"

"Feel like?"

"Yes."

"I once saw the actor John Travolta do an interview on TV where he described doing research for the movie he played a junkie," Ellen said. "He said a recovering heroin junkie told him to get drunk on Tequila and float on your back in a warm pool. Being on heroin is a thousand times better than that."

"And is it?"

"Oh yeah," Ellen said.

"Worth dying over?"

"When you're on it, worth killing over."

"Thanks for the info," I said. "It helps with the mindset."

"You're trying to understand how a man can kill a woman and steal a baby to buy money for drugs?" Ellen said.

"It helps to understand the man I'll be hunting," I said.

"I guess hunting is a good word to describe it," Ellen said.

We arrived at the lot. I parked at my usual spot and walked Ellen to her car.

"I'll be in touch soon," I said.

Ellen opened the door and slid into the seat. "I enjoyed talking to you Mr. Kellerman. I mean Kellerman. Good night."

"Good night."

After Ellen drove away, I crossed the street and went up to my apartment. I heard music coming from Mrs. Parker's apartment.

I knocked on her door.

The door opened with the chain in place.

"Mr. Kellerman, is everything alright?" Mrs. Parker asked.

"Fine. Do you still have that box that allows you to watch movies?"

"It's called Netflix, Mr. Kellerman, and yes I still have it."

"I'd like to watch a movie tomorrow if that's possible?"

"What time?"

"Afternoon. I'll order out lunch. What would you like?

"Chinese from the place around the corner. Make it around one-thirty," Mrs. Parker said. "I have to watch my soaps first."

"Okay."

I went to my apartment where the cats greeted me at the door. I fed and watered them and after a petting session on the bed, I turned in early.

I made a mental to do list and then drifted off to sleep.

A noise woke me a few hours later. The cats heard it too and bounced off the bed and ran to the door. I slid open the drawer in the night stand and removed the .357 Magnum revolver and silencer I keep there for emergency use. I attached the silencer and as quietly as possible, I went to the living room.

I stood to the right of the door and waited.

So did the cats. They sat in front of the door and looked at it.

Silent minutes passed and then I heard the faint click of a key sliding into the lock. It slid to the point it was fully inserted, but the key didn't turn.

I waited.

The cats waited.

The key slid out of the lock. Footsteps echoed softly on the tiled hallway floor.

I lowered the .357.

The cats looked at me.

I hit the light switch on the wall, went to the sofa, set the .357 on the coffee table, grabbed my smokes and lit one. The cats jumped on the sofa and began a mutual grooming session.

The only person on earth who had a key to my apartment door is Maria. I had given her one and one for the lobby years ago. The cats recognized her scent as well.

I looked at the clock on the wall. Just past three in the morning.

I went to the window and looked down at the dark street. A car was parked across the street by a hydrant. A woman wearing a dark trench coat and a hat emerged from my building and crossed the street. She went to the passenger door of the parked car and opened the door.

As she got in, I could see the person behind the wheel was a woman, but the interior lights went out and I couldn't see faces.

Maria and her lover?

What did they want at three in the morning that couldn't wait?

Chapter Seven

After a light breakfast at the coffee shop, I pounded out a ninety minute workout at the Y and was back in my apartment by ten.

I showered, changed and went to see Mrs. Parker.

"Two things," I said. "First, call the locksmith and change the lock for the lobby door and second I need the phone for a moment."

"Did something happen?" she asked.

"Precaution," I said. "I saw some junkies hanging around. I want a better lock for the door."

She nodded and handed me the phone.

I sat on the stairs and called Hawkins.

"Prepare a typed letter of introduction for me as an employee of your firm working as an investigator," I said.

"Stop by this afternoon and pick it up," Hawkins said.

"Thanks."

I returned the phone to Mrs. Parker.

"See you later with Chinese," I said.

I hit the library for a quick session at a computer. Even though I don't own a computer, I belonged to several browsing sites for background checks. I checked the remaining twelve names from Ellen's list for arrest records and prison terms.

Four of the twelve were serving time. Two in Jersey, one in upstate New York, one in Pennsylvania.

I printed copies of the four incarcerated and called it a day.

I walked to the Chinese restaurant on Tenth Avenue and ordered a hundred dollars worth of takeout. Thirty minutes later, I carried two large shopping bags back to the apartment.

"Are we having company?" Mrs. Parker asked as she unpacked the shopping bags.

"Just us. I wasn't sure what you wanted so I got everything."

"What movie?"

"Drugstore Cowboy."

Mrs. Parker downloaded the movie onto her forty-eight-inch flat screen television and we went to work on the Chinese as we watched the movie.

The plot was simple enough. Junkies in Kansas City do whatever it takes to stay high and one step ahead of the law. Some of them die, one finds redemption, and one offered to get clean decides getting high is more fun than getting straight.

It was a well-acted film and portrayed the desperation of the junkies in a realistic way. Showed their desperation and despair and how it ruined family life.

"There's enough leftovers for a week," Mrs. Parker said.

"Put what you think the cats would like in a small bowl," I said. "I'll pick it up later."

*****

Hawkins me the neatly typed letter authorizing me to act as a special investigator for his law firm.

We sat at his conference table and had coffee.

I removed the printed documents I got at the library and gave them to Hawkins.

"Contact the prisons and make an appointment for me to interview them," I said.

"And they are?"

"Old friends of Brian Cosby."

Hawkins nodded. "Hence the letter of introduction."

"Hence."

"Any particular order?"

"New York, Jersey, Pennsylvania."

"Stop by tomorrow afternoon."

"Can I use your phone before I go?" I said.

*****

I parked my car in Ellen's driveway. She wasn't home from work yet. I smoked a cigarette as I waited. She said she had a client meeting and might be a bit late.

Just after six, she pulled into the driveway and parked next to the Lincoln.

We both got out.

Ellen wore a blue skirt with a matching jacket over a white blouse and high heels. A simple string of pearls garnished her neck.

We walked to the door.

"As long as you're here, want to stay for dinner?" she asked.

"Were you cooking anyway?" I asked as we entered her house.

"Frozen entrée."

"Any good restaurants around?"

"A few. I'll need to change."

"Change. We can talk shop over dinner."

"Are you in a hurry? I need a shower."

"Take your time."

I went to the kitchen, opened the sliding door and sat at the patio table. I was on a second cigarette when Ellen slid open the doors and joined me.

She had changed into designer jeans with an expensive looking sweatshirt and black walking shoes. Her hair was still damp from the shower.

"We'll take my car, okay?" she said.

*****

Ellen drove us to the Roma Italian restaurant on the boardwalk of Staten Island. It's really named the Franklin D. Roosevelt Boardwalk, but nobody ever calls it that. It stretches about two and a half miles along the beach and took a pounding during the hurricane a few years back. Quite a few stores and shops were still closed from that event.

We settled on an outside table facing the dark ocean. It was a warm night and the moon would soon be up.

Ellen ordered chicken parm. I went with the veal parm. She had water with lemon. I ordered Coke with ice.

I produced a copy of the list of four.

"What can you tell me about these four?" I asked.

Ellen read the names. "Oh boy," she said. "It doesn't surprise me they're in prison. What surprises me is it's only four."

"Let's go down the list," I said.

"John Pietrie," Ellen said. "He was a junkie through and through. He'd sell him mother into slavery for a fix. I believe he went to high school with Brian and they started using at the same time. Violent bastard. His favorite way to get money was to roll gay drunks. Brian would pick up a guy in a gay bar and Pietrie would roll him on the way to the car. He scared me most of the time. I begged Brian to ditch him, but Brian said he was a good earner."

The waitress brought us our drinks.

"Next," I said.

"Steve Maples," Ellen said. "Older than Brian at the time. He was a longtime user with a lot of connections. He didn't travel with us but more than once he set up a place for us to stay on the road."

"Next."

"Andy Davis," Ellen said. "A quiet kid. I always had the feeling he hated being a junkie, but he lacked the will to quit. He was an excellent thief. He specialized in home burglary. He traveled with us sometimes if the cops were after him."

"Last."

"Bradley Coopersmith," Ellen said. "Came from money. Had a fifty-thousand-dollar a year trust fund that he usually went through by April and spent the rest of the year hustling. He was a funny gut actually and knew a thousand jokes. He traveled with us sometimes. He wanted to get straight and talked about it sometimes, but I thought he lacked the will."

The waitress returned with dinner.

We continued talking as we ate.

"After I finish with these four, we talk about the remaining eight," I said.

Ellen nodded. "Do you have a photographic memory?" she asked.

"I've never had it tested," I said. "I've always just be able to remember things without having to take many notes."

"When are you seeing these four?" Ellen asked.

"In a day or two."

"Do you think there might be a connection?"

"I'm shaking a tree to see what falls out," I said. "I watched that movie."

"Drugstore Cowboy? What did you think?"

"I didn't care for the ending," I said. "I don't like when the ending is left to interpretation. The star is either dead or alive. It needs to be spelled out. I felt sorry for the woman at the end."

"Because she chose to remain a junkie rather than get straight?"

"I think her character really wanted to get straight but she lacked the inner strength to go through with it," I said. "Also the priest was a pretty pathetic character."

"Go to enough AA meetings and you meet quite a few priests and nuns taking the pledge," Ellen said.

We finished dinner and had room for dessert. Coffee and chocolate cheesecake.

"Ever stroll this boardwalk?" Ellen asked on the way to her Bronco.

"I'm not a beach goer type of guy," I said.

Ellen took my arm. "Let's walk a bit."

We walked a bit, maybe a quarter of a mile. There were some benches facing the water. The moon was up and shimmering off the ocean. We sat for a few minutes and I smoked a cigarette.

"What did you do before you did this?" Ellen asked.

"I was in the Marine Corps," I said.

"That doesn't surprise me," Ellen said. "Why did you leave?"

"I didn't. They left me."

"I'm not … what does that mean?"

"They kicked me out," I said. "Me and a buddy. We were on guard duty at the Iraqi oil wells. Some Army assholes took it upon themselves to capture and rape some local women. Kurds. We were supposed to be protecting these people and here we were raping the women. My friend and I killed all five of those rapist bastards. My buddy and I were arrested and spent a year in the brig while the Pentagon figured out what to do with us. They finally decided to spare the publicity of a public trial and ruin the image of the military and discharged us and erased our military records. They did give us a year's back pay, though. I thought that was right considerable of them."

"Wow," Ellen said. "That's quite a story. Would you do it again?"

"And not think twice," I said. "Some people just don't deserve to live. Those soldiers were the worst kind of men who join the military."

"What kinds are there?"

I inhaled and blew a smoke ring. "The kind who joins because they want to take advantage of the college benefits afterward. Then the kind that are escaping poverty and need a job. There's the kind who believe in their country and want to help. Then there are those who join because they want the legal means to kill somebody. Those five soldiers were that kind."

"What kind were you?"

"Number three."

"And now?"

"I believe in me."

Ellen nodded. "I need to get home," she said. "It's quarterly tax season and I have an eight o'clock appointment tomorrow morning."

"Sure."

I waited beside my car until Ellen was safely in the house before I drove home. I took the long way opting for the Verazzano Narrows Bridge to Brooklyn and then the Brooklyn Bridge to Manhattan.

I used the time to think and sort out some details. It was after one when I parked the Lincoln in the lot. The guard in the shack handed me an envelope as I walked past him.

From Mrs. Parker was handwritten on the envelope. Inside was a new set of keys.

The Bar and Grill didn't close until two and I ducked inside where Johnny was behind the bar. A few last minute drinkers were scattered among tables and stools at the bar.

"What's your poison?" Johnny asked as I grabbed a stool.

"Sprite with lemon," I said.

Johnny served it up and poured a shot of bourbon for himself.

"Your Mrs. Parker came in to see me about some keys," Johnny said. "I told her to leave it at the lot."

"I got them."

"Trouble in the building?"

I told Johnny what happened the other night with Maria.

"It appears Davis is correct," Johnny said.

"Appears so."

"Would you like the competition to go away?" Johnny asked.

"No."

Johnny nodded. "Even gone it wouldn't be gone I suppose."

"No."

"Any progress with Miss Fallen?"

"Too soon to tell," I said.

"I'll keep the check in the safe," Johnny said.

I nodded.

"I have a small favor to ask," Johnny said.

"Sure."

"The annual Hell's Kitchen Block Party is next week."

"Aw shit," I said.

"You'll do it."

"I owe you one I suppose."

Johnny grinned at me.

"Yes, you do," he said.

"Fuck," I said.

Chapter Eight

"Three letters of introduction and I've already spoken with the wardens of all prisons involved," Hawkins said.

I looked at the three envelopes on his desk and picked them up and slipped them into my jacket pocket.

"What?" Hawkins said as I stood there.

"If nothing pans out, I'd like you to do something for me," I said.

"Will it get me disbarred?" Hawkins joked.

"Yes," I said.

Hawkins stared at me.

"But only if you get caught," I said. "I'll get back to you after I see the two upstate tomorrow."

"Wait," Hawkins said as I left his office. "You're kidding about disbarred, right?"

I grinned to myself in the elevator and all the way to my car parked in a lot on Thirty-First Street.

*****

I spent the afternoon in Roth's Gym. After thirty minutes on the speed bag, another thirty on the heavy bag I took a seat ringside with Roth and watched a pair of bums dance around the ring.

"If you're waiting for the next Sugar Ray or Ali to walk through your doors, you'll be dead and buried," I said.

"Fuck," Roth said.

*****

I was about to step in the shower when Mrs. Parker knocked on my door.

"Message," she said.

I wrapped a towel around my waist and went to the door.

"From Maria," Mrs. Parker said and handed me a note.

"Thanks."

I sat on the sofa and read the note.

Come to dinner tonight. We need to talk.

*****

Maria answered the door wearing black jeans, a white blouse and black socks. Her dark hair was pinned up and she wore little if any makeup.

"Want to talk in the house or backyard?" she asked.

"Backyard."

We walked through the living room to the kitchen where she put on slippers and then we went out to the patio table.

A pot of coffee with two cups was on the table.

"I figured you'd say outside so you can smoke," Maria said.

"When did you ever say I couldn't smoke inside?" I asked.

Maria shrugged. "It smells cleaner."

I filled both cups and sat.

"To who?" I asked.

Maria sat and looked at me. "Where to begin?" she said.

"Why not start with when you decided to dump me and become a lesbian?" I said.

"I didn't ... I'm not ... look, I'm going through a tough time right now," Maria said. "Prison is ..."

"I know what prison is," I said. "I could have let this house foreclose and your car go to auction. I paid all your legal bills and kept you from a fifteen year manslaughter stretch. In return I get dumped for not another man but a woman. You owe me nothing, not even an explanation, but it would be nice to hear one anyway."

I lit a smoke and drank some coffee.

Maria went to that place somewhere between anger and tears.

"It takes one to know one," she finally said.

"One what?"

"Lonely, confused woman used by men all her life."

"I never used you," I said. "I would have married you on a dime if you weren't always so worried about your precious career as a cop."

"Every man in power on the force used me from the first day," Maria said. "It's how I wound up in jail."

"I know. I was there every step of the way."

"I know that."

"So you met a fellow man-hater in prison and decided to cut me out and cut her in," I said.

"It's not that simple."

"Nothing ever is," I said.

"No."

"Tell me about her."

"She's … like me in a way," Maria said. "Used and abused by the system and men. She was married and got tired of being beaten up by him and decided to do something about it. She bought a gun on the street and the next time he hit her she shot him. She didn't kill him though. She was arrested for illegal possession and sentenced to two years. One for the possession, the other for the shooting. We met six months ago when she was transferred to West Virginia. We started out as acquaintances, then friends and finally …"

"Lovers?"

"It's not how you might think."

"And how is that?"

"Angry man-hating lesbians with a closetful of sex toys," Maria said. "It's very sweet and soft."

"So is vanilla custard."

Maria sighed.

"So why did you come to my apartment during the night?" I asked. "Why did you want to talk to me?"

"That's why you changed the locks, huh?"

I blew smoke and nodded.

Maria sighed. "I hate to admit this, but I still want and need what's between your legs."

"I don't share, especially your honey pot and especially with a woman," I said.

Maria's eyes went dark as storm clouds. It only lasted for a few moments and then she softened.

"What if …?"

"There are no what ifs in my world," I said. "Only what is. You're either my woman or you aren't. It's that simple."

"Why can't I be your woman and …?"

"I told you, I don't share."

"Why do you have to be so damned parochial?"

"Parochial?"

"It means …"

"I know what it means," I said. "If I was interested in a threesome I would have crossed that bridge a long time ago."

"There is no talking to you," Maria said.

"We're talking right now," I said. "I'm just not saying what you want to hear."

"I have some photos of you in the house," Maria said. "I showed them to her. Know what she said?"

"I really don't give a rat's ass what she said. So unless you have anything else to say, I'll be running along."

Maria stared at me.

I dropped the cigarette in the coffee cup and went around the garden to the front to my car.

*****

"How many cops did you hire for security?" I asked Johnny.

"Six. Same as last year."

"The why do you need me?"

"Same reason as last year," Johnny said. "The cops watch the money and you watch the cops."

"Shit."

Behind the bar, Johnny tossed back a shot of bourbon and refilled the glass.

I sipped my coffee and zoned out for a few minutes.

"You seem preoccupied," Johnny said.

"Maria contacted me. She wanted to talk."

"And?"

"She wants me to share."

"With the other woman?"

I nodded.

"And you said?"

"No, of course."

"Because the thought of two women sitting on your face frightens you?"

I had to grin. Johnny was the only man I'd allow to talk to me like that and he knew it.

"I'm going home," I said. "I have a long drive tomorrow."

"Don't forget next Thursday and Friday."

"If I do, you'll remind me," I said.

Chapter Nine

I was out of bed early, grabbed a quick breakfast at the coffee shop and then hit the weight room at the Y for an hour and ran for thirty minutes on the indoor track afterward.

Back in the apartment, I shaved, showered and put on a lightweight tan suit with a blue tie and black loafers. Because they expected it, I wore the Browning .45 in a belt holster that served me well for fifteen years.

The two hour plus drive was broken up by a quick bite at a highway rest stop. I grabbed a burger with fries and a Coke and read the sports section of the Daily News.

Once back on the road, I drove the remaining eighty miles in under an hour and arrived at the prison just before one in the afternoon.

After a guard read the letter from Hawkins and I checked my gun, I met briefly with the warden to clear the sessions.

I was given a one hour time limit with each prisoner.

I was escorted to a conference room where lawyers meet with clients. After fifteen minutes, John Pietrie was brought in by two guards. He was in chains. They removed the chains and cuffed his right arm to the steel loop on the table.

The guards went to the door to stand watch.

"I don't know you," Pietrie said.

"No. Want something to drink?"

"Coke or Pepsi would be good."

I waved to a guard and he came over.

"Can we get two Cokes?"

He nodded and left the room.

Pietrie used his left hand to reach into his right shirt pocket and bring out a pack of cigarettes and a book of matches.

"Can you light one for me?" he asked.

I used my lighter to light his and then one of my own.

"Thanks."

"Know why I'm here?" I asked.

"The warden told me you're looking for Brian Cosby."

"Actually, I don't give a fuck about Brian Cosby," I said. "But he has a ten-year-old son somewhere that stands to inherit a substantial sum of money if I can find him."

"No shit. Well, good for the kid," Pietrie said.

"So if I find Cosby maybe I can find the kid."

Pietrie inhaled on his cigarette. His bio listed him as forty-years-old, but he looked a decade or more older. He was tall, but thin as most addicts are. Somewhere in there I could see he once played sports, but that was long ago.

"I got two years to go on my stretch," Pietrie said. "I've been clean for thirty-six months now. When I get out of here I'm going to live with my mother in Florida. Since I will do my full time I won't be on parole and can go where I please. My uncle, my Ma's brother owns a carpet cleaning business in Miami-Dade and he's got a job waiting for me. I'm telling you this because I have no desire to return to the 'life' so to speak. I did a lot of bad things, hurt a lot of people and my Ma is almost seventy and deserves some peace."

"So let's talk about Brian Cosby," I said. "And I make sure you get five cartons of cigarettes when I leave."

"I appreciate that," Pietrie said.

"When did you last see him?"

"Got to be five years ago," Pietrie said. "Hoboken, I think. No, that's not right. Trenton. He has a girlfriend. Ellen somebody. My memory isn't what it should be. It's a wonder I can remember anything at all."

"I'm not so interested in where Cosby was as in where he might be," I said.

"You mean now?"

I nodded.

"Is he even alive?"

"I don't know," I said. "If he was, where would he go to disappear?"

Pietrie shook his head. "We traveled together moving around to stay ahead of the cops, but we didn't really know each other all that well. You got to remember a junkie's primary interest is scoring enough drugs to stay high."

The guard returned with two cans of Coke.

"Thanks," I said.

I popped the tabs and we both sipped.

I lit a cigarette and waited.

"See a junkie learns to stay ahead of the cops and blend in and become invisible," Pietrie said. "Since the only goal is to continue getting high you have to learn to survive."

I sipped some Coke.

"Where did you last see Cosby five years ago?" I asked. "Was it Hoboken or Trenton and did he have a girlfriend with him or was he alone?"

"I'm thinking," Pietrie said.

I smoked and sipped while Pietrie thought.

"Lewiston, Maine and he was alone," Pietrie said. "Five years ago. That was the last time I saw him."

"You're sure?"

Pietrie nodded.

"A lot of heroin on the streets in Lewiston," Pietrie said. "Easy access with tons of places to hide and shoot up. Heroin is as easy to get as candy up there. We met by accident in the abandoned warehouse by this river. Must have been twenty others inside all getting high."

"And was alone?"

Pietrie nodded. "I remember I asked him where his girl was and he said he ditched her years ago. Said something like she was becoming a drag and it was safer to travel alone. We slept off the high in the warehouse and in the morning he was gone. I never saw him again after that. I started traveling with this guy from Albany. I don't remember his name. That's where I got busted, in Albany. Mugged a little old lady and hurt her pretty bad. I wish I knew if she was still alive. I'd like to apologize to her for what I did."

"Anything else?"

Pietrie shook his head. "Maybe I'll remember more later."

I waved to a guard and he approached the table. I dug out a business card for Hawkins and showed the guard.

"I'm giving him this business card in case he remembers something and needs to call me," I said.

The guard inspected the card and nodded.

"Five cartons will be delivered to your cell," I said to Pietrie.

He nodded. "Thank you."

*****

I took a break, grabbed a coffee in the prison lounge and went outside for some fresh air and a smoke.

Then I met with Andy Davis.

He was short, thin, with mousey brown hair and rimless glasses. Behind the glasses, his dull blue eyes looked at me. Once he was secured to the loop, he said, "I don't place you."

"That's because we've never met," I said.

"They told me you wanted to talk about Brian Cosby, I figured we met or why else would you want to see me?" Davis said.

"I work for a law firm and I'm looking for Cosby," I said. "I understand you two traveled around a lot in the past."

"We did I suppose."

"Well, he vanished about seven years ago and I need to find him."

"Why?"

"Did you know he had a son?"

"I did not," Davis said. "Hey, what do you think?"

He smiled to display a beautiful set of white teeth.

"I had bad gum disease," Davis said. "All junkies do. The prison dentist yanked them all out and made me a full set of dentures."

"They look very nice," I said. "So when did you last see Brian Cosby?"

"Lemme think a second."

"Take your time."

"I've been in here three years now," Davis said. "I get out in twenty-three months you know."

I dug out my smokes and lit one.

"I had to quit those," Davis said. "They were yellowing my new teeth."

"Use a whitening toothpaste," I said. "About Cosby?"

"I dunno man," Davis said. "I can't remember. It was a while ago."

As is common with junkies, Davis was having difficulty with his memory.

"Would you have any chocolate?" he asked.

"No."

"I love chocolate."

"I'll have some sent to your cell," I said.

"Really. That's very nice of you."

"Sure."

"You said he had a kid, huh?"

"I did."

"Well, it never came up last I saw him if that helps."

"It does," I said. "What kind of chocolate do you like?"

*****

"So you struck out?" Hawkins said.

"Not completely," I said. "We know that Cosby was seen in Maine two years after his son was born. That means he didn't entirely vanish seven years ago."

"Five years is still a long time to account for," Hawkins said.

"I checked arrest and death records," I said. "If he was arrested or died, maybe it was under an assumed name."

"Possible."

"Things fall through the cracks."

"They do."

We were at the conference table in Hawkins's office. I picked up the phone and dialed Ellen's number.

"It's Kellerman," I said when she picked up.

"Hello Kellerman," she said.

"I need you to do something for me," I said. "Another list. Write down all the fake names Cosby used over the years, as many as you can remember. I'll stop by tomorrow after you get off work."

"Tomorrow is Saturday."

"So it is," I said.

"Come by around six," Ellen said. "I'll fix a real dinner."

"Okay."

After I hung up, Hawkins said, "I'd like to see that list. Maybe I can run down the names quicker than you calling in a few favors."

"I'll drop it off on Monday," I said.

"I've been thinking about that favor you mentioned," Hawkins said.

"Keep thinking."

*****

A dark haired beauty wearing black pants and a white blouse was sitting on the steps of my building when I parked the car in the lot and crossed the street.

She stood as I approached the steps.

"You're Kellerman. I recognize you from your picture. You're bigger in person," she said.

"And you are?"

"Denise. I'd like to talk with you if you have a moment."

"About?"

"Maria, what else?"

"I'll give you the time it takes to drink a cup of coffee," I said. "Want to come up or go down the street?"

"Maria said you have cats. I'm allergic to cats."

*****

The waitress at the coffee shop filled our cups, smiled and walked away.

"I just want you to know Maria didn't send me," Denise said. "I'm here on my own."

"And you want what?"

"She wants you back," Denise said. "What we have is very special, but she still needs a man in her life."

"Enough to give you up?" I asked. "Enough for you to give her up?"

"Why does anybody have to give anybody up?" Denise asked.

"Look, I'm happy that you make each other happy and have something special, but I'll tell you what I told her, I'm not a sharing kind of guy," I said. "I want for little, but what's mine is mine and I don't share it."

Denise stared at me.

"End of story," I said.

Chapter Ten

I hit the weight room at the Y for an hour, skipped the track and jogged the mile through the streets to Roth's Gym.

The old man was ringside watching a pair of welterweights spar when I arrived. He waved me over.

"Waddaya think?" Roth asked.

I studied the two fighters for a few moments.

"The kid in green drops his left when he throws his right and the kid in blue flinches every time he thinks he's going to get hit," I said.

"Fuck," Roth said.

I left him and went to the wall and removed a jump rope. After fifteen minutes, I worked the speed bag for thirty minutes and then another thirty on the heavy bag. Afterward I returned to the ring where Roth was screaming at two cumbersome heavyweights.

"Look at these fat tubs of shit," Roth said. "You could knock the both of them out at the same time in half a round."

"Want me to?" I said.

"Naw, I ain't in the mood for cleaning up blood," Roth said.

*****

I filled the tub with hot water and Epsom salts and soaked with a mug of coffee and a cigarette.

The cats sat on the tiled floor and watched me with keen interest.

I analyzed the meetings with Pietrie and Davis. I learned that Cosby was alive as recently as five years ago, but five years is a long time to account for.

I wouldn't see Coopersmith and Maples until Monday and Tuesday at the earliest, but at best the meetings would go the same.

When the water went cold, I drained the tub and took a hot shower.

*****

Ellen answered her door wearing tan slacks with a white sweatshirt. She wore white socks without shoes.

"I just made coffee," she said as I followed her to the kitchen.

Fried chicken was crackling in a large cast iron pan,

"It's almost done," Ellen said. "My mother's recipe. I haven't made it since I don't know when."

I grabbed a mug off the counter and filled it from the pot.

"Anything I can do?" I asked.

"The potatoes are mashed and keeping hot. Same with the carrots. Do you know how to whip cream?"

"I do."

"Then after we eat you can whip the cream," Ellen said. "I made an apple crisp for dessert."

I nodded and took a seat at the table.

"You can smoke," Ellen said as she turned the chicken.

*****

"That was the best fried chicken I've ever had," I said.

"If it is you can thank my mother," Ellen said. "I'll clear the table and you get started on the whipped cream and we can talk shop at the patio table. It's a warm night."

There was a large steel mixing bowl in the fridge beside a quart of heavy whipping cream.

"You can use the electric beater or the hand-held," Ellen said. "The hand-held takes longer but whips a better peak."

I opted for the hand-held and poured the cream into the bowl and got to work. Using the hand-held it took about ten minutes before the cream started to form peaks, but Ellen was right, they were larger and stiffer than whipped cream I usually got in restaurants.

By that time, Ellen had set the table in the backyard. Bowls of apple crisp with fresh coffee. She took the bowl of cream and lathered the apple crisp.

"Now we can talk shop," she said.

I told her about the meetings with Pietrie and Davis.

"So we know Brian was alive up until five years ago," Ellen said. "I'm impressed."

"Five years is a long time," I said. "What about the list I asked you to make."

"I'll get it."

She went inside for a moment and returned with a legal pad.

"As far as I can remember, Brian used these names to hide himself under," Ellen said. "There is probably a lot more I'm unaware of."

I counted twenty-nine names on the sheet.

"I'll get started on this right away," I said.

Ellen nodded. "Would you … would you like to go to a meeting with me at nine?"

"I don't have anything else to do," I said.

*****

Ellen drove us to a Baptist church about a mile from her home. The meeting lasted just over an hour and took place in the basement. Thirty plus were in attendance. Besides the chairperson, four people from the group shared their stories.

Ellen had us back at her place by ten thirty.

"Come in for a minute," Ellen said. "I thought of a few additional names for the list."

We sat at the kitchen table with glasses of caffeine free Coke.

"If I have any caffeine after eight I'm up half the night," Ellen said. "Smoke if you want to, it won't bother me."

I lit one up and watched as Ellen wrote five names on the legal pad.

"I thought I had another six, but I guess it's only five," she said.

She tore off the sheet and slid it across the table.

"I'll find out anyway, but are any of these names real people?" I asked.

"Hard for me to say," Ellen said. "As far as I know I've never met any of them, but Brian knew a lot of people. The only reason I even remember so many is over seven years he used these names mostly for hotels and when meeting new dealers and things like that."

I nodded. "Monday and Tuesday, I'll be meeting with Coopersmith and Maples," I said. "We'll touch base on Wednesday."

"Okay."

Ellen walked me to the door. "Thanks for going to the meeting with me."

"Thanks for dinner."

I wasn't sure what time the last ferry for Manhattan left, but I was in the mood to drive and took the Verazzano to Brooklyn and then the Brooklyn Bridge to Manhattan.

I was home and in bed by one-thirty.

Except that I couldn't sleep.

When I finally gave up trying, I went to the kitchen, poured a glass of milk, sat at the table with the list Ellen gave me and studied it.

Some of the names Cosby used were obvious. Some were not. Most amateurs are afraid they won't remember their fake names and use a form of their real name scrambled. Brian Cosby becomes Bruce Colby or Brendon Cross.

The cats decided to get in on things and jumped onto the table and began rubbing me. I scratched their backs and ears until they had enough and they went to the window.

I looked at the list one more time, felt sleep was ready to take over and returned to bed.

Chapter Eleven

I usually take Sunday off from the gym to allow my body to recoup. Mrs. Parker knocked on my door around nine-thirty.

"I'm going to make breakfast, would you care to join me?" she asked.

"I have a better idea," I said. "Why not let me take you out for breakfast."

"Out? You mean to a restaurant?"

"That's what I mean."

"My hair is a mess."

"It's fine."

"What do I wear?"

"Whatever you want."

"Give me thirty minutes."

"No problem."

*****

"When you said breakfast out I thought we would walk," Mrs. Parker said as I drove across the Brooklyn Bridge.

"Ever been to Junior's?" I said.

"I don't think so. Is that where we're going?"

"It is."

"Is it expensive? I have to watch my budget."

"When I take a woman out on a date, I always pay," I said.

"A date Mr. Kellerman, really."

I grinned.

"It's quite a view, isn't it?" Mrs. Parker said.

"It is, but the 59th Street Bridge is better," I said.

After crossing the bridge, I skirted neighborhood streets to Junior's Restaurant located on Flatbush Avenue. It's a massive place known throughout the country for its cheesecake. The line was out the door, but the restaurant's size kept the wait to a minimum.

Once we were seated at a table for two, Mrs. Parker was like a kid in a candy store. She ordered nearly everything on the breakfast menu while I went with a stack of pancakes with bacon.

"How on earth do you weigh only a hundred pounds?" I asked as I marveled at the way she put food away.

"I follow a simple rule I made for myself fifty years ago after my second child came," she said. "I eat twice a day twelve hours apart. If I get hungry after this feast we're having, I'll wait until midnight to eat something."

"It's a good rule."

"It's served me well," Mrs. Parker said. "I'll be eighty-one next month and I don't weigh any more than I did fifty years ago."

"Did you save room for dessert?"

She ordered a huge slice of chocolate cheesecake smothered in strawberries and whipped cream. I didn't have the room, but ordered the same.

"Mr. Kellerman, I don't mean to pry, but what's become of that lovely woman you used to see all the time?" she asked.

"For want of a better word, she dumped me," I said.

"Heavens sake, why?"

"It's a long and unimportant story," I said.

"That's why you wanted the lock changed. She has a key."

"Like I said, it's unimportant," I said.

*****

"Are you in a hurry to get home?" I asked when we were back in the car.

"Not particularly."

"Good."

I skirted across Brooklyn and took the BQE into Queens and then over to Long Island City and hooked up with the 59th Street Bridge. It's actually named the Queensborough Bridge, but I can't remember the last time I heard it called that.

"Ever crossed this bridge?" I asked Mrs. Parker as we began to cross.

"Not that I remember."

"Then just watch."

As we drove across the bridge, around the midpoint the Manhattan skyline becomes a glorious moving postcard of the city.

I heard Mrs. Parker take a breath and hold it.

"It's ... beautiful," she said, finally exhaling.

*****

"Your son lives in Queens, doesn't he?" I asked Mrs. Parker as she unlocked her door.

"He does. My daughter moved to Florida."

I nodded. "I think I'll take a nap and sleep off brunch."

Mrs. Parker took my arm. "Mr. Kellerman, thank you."

"Welcome."

I waddled into my apartment and found the cats asleep on the bed. I stripped down and joined them.

When I awoke it was dark outside.

I grabbed a quick shower, dressed and went down to the Bar to play a few games of chess with Johnny.

The first game ended in a draw.

During the second game, Johnny said, "The police have been arranged for block party. Six detectives. This year the Ferris Wheel is sixteen stories high. That's a hundred and sixty feet."

"How much did it raise for charity last year?" I asked.

"The books say one hundred and forty thousand," Johnny said.

"How much was skimmed?"

"Hard to say," Johnny said. "Maybe twenty-five thousand."

"How much do the cops get for special detail?"

"Thirty-eight and hour."

"And that's not enough," I said.

"To some people there is no such word as enough."

"Maybe this year they learn," I said.

"Maybe," Johnny said as he slid his queen across the board. "Check," he said.

I studied the board.

"Goddammit," I said.

Chapter Twelve

After a ninety minute workout at the Y, I walked home and took a quick shave and shower.

The workouts weren't the same without Davis. We pushed each other to the brink and that competition between us was missing and I often felt flat as if I was just going through the motions.

I was in Hawkins's office by eleven o'clock.

He scanned the list of names. "Shouldn't be too difficult for the police to cross check this in the system," he said. "I'll tell my contacts it's a missing heir case, which technically it is."

"Anything on Davis yet?" I asked.

"I'll be filing papers by the end of the week."

"Does he know?"

"I was hoping you would save me the trip."

*****

"What you want?" Davis asked by telephone.

I looked at him through the glass. "Remember Hawkins?"

"I remember."

"He's filing early release papers on you."

"Good. I get to kill you that much sooner."

"You look like shit," I said. "I'll make a deal with you. When you get out, you let me get you into shape. I'd hate to be killed by a flabby assassin."

"You crazy."

"Of course I am," I said. "Otherwise I would have had you killed in there by now. Give me six months to whip you back into shape and then you'll have a fighting chance when you come for me."

"Don't gotta be in shape to pull a trigger," Davis said.

"If you refuse my offer, you won't see next week," I said. "Take it or leave it. Take it and when you get out we train together for six months. Leave it and the prison is short one inmate before next week. Choose."

"You not crazy you insane," Davis said.

"Watch your back," I said and hung up the phone.

As I stood, Davis pounded on the glass.

I lifted the phone.

"I take your deal on one condition," Davis said. "After six months, no guns, no weapons, just you and me."

"Now who's crazy," I said.

"Yes or no?"

"Yes," I said. "Is there anything you need in there?"

"Books. I'll make a list and give it to you next time you decide to visit."

*****

"Can he beat you?" Johnny asked as he studied the chess board.

"No," I said. "Even when he was in top shape he couldn't take me one-on-one."

"The question is how far are you willing to go?" Johnny asked.

"If you mean will I kill him the answer is no," I said.

Johnny slid his queen and placed my knight in jeopardy. "If you leave him alive he will come back with a gun," he said.

I studied the board. If I moved the knight my king would be in check and three moves later in checkmate.

"I've invested too much time in you to allow him to shoot you in the back like a dog," Johnny said.

I backed my king up to safety and Johnny took my knight.

"A bridge can't be crossed until you come to it," I said.

"What is that, some Oscar Wilde bullshit?" Johnny asked.

"Chinese fortune cookie from takeout last week," I said.

Johnny grinned and slid a bishop into position. "Chinese food gives me heartburn," he said.

Cindy left the bar and came to the table.

"Lieutenant Sullivan called," she said. "He'll be by in a few minutes."

Johnny nodded.

Cindy returned to the bar.

"Stick around," Johnny said.

I studied the board for a few minutes and then toppled my king.

"Let's go to the office," Johnny said.

*****

Sullivan stood six-foot-four and weighed a good two-fifty. A career cop, he ran a vice squad on the West Side and, as they say, never made a soft arrest. He never passed up a free drink or meal and had the reputation for violence, especially against hookers and pimps.

"Who the fuck is this?" he asked when Cindy brought him into the office.

"One of the block party organizers," Johnny said.

Johnny had a glass of his bourbon. The bottle was on the desk along with another glass.

Sullivan lifted the bottle and filled the glass to the rim and swallowed half in several gulps. "The news is the rates for private detail went up ten an hour," he said.

"The event is for charity," Johnny said.

Sullivan polished off the rest of his glass and refilled it. "We all know where charity begins, don't we, Johnny?" he said.

"Forty-eight an hour is a lot of money for six cops to stand around all night doing nothing," Johnny said.

"It is what it is," Sullivan said. "You want the detail or not?"

"Seems I have no choice as it's a city requirement," Johnny said.

"No, you don't." Sullivan looked at me. I was against the file cabinet looking at him. "Something you looking at, pal?" he said.

I shook my head.

"So six men plus myself at forty-eight an hour," Sullivan said.

"You didn't charge for yourself last year," Johnny said.

"Last year," Sullivan said.

He swallowed the second glass of bourbon and set the glass on the desk. "Wednesday night then," he said.

After Sullivan left, Johnny looked at me and nodded slightly.

"How about another game?" I said.

Chapter Thirteen

Steven Maples looked at me from across the table in the meeting room.

"You don't look like a lawyer," he said.

"I'm not a lawyer," I said. "I'm an investigator for a law firm. We're looking for Brian Cosby and I understand that you know him."

"The first fucking thing I'm gonna do when I leave this Jersey shithole is find a dealer that sells Afghan madman and get high for a fucking week and eat Doritos by the bag," Maples said.

"My sources tell me you once set up a safe house for Cosby and his girlfriend," I said.

"Got any chocolate?"

"No."

"For each question you ask me you gotta get me one chocolate bar," Maples said. "And no one ounce bar shit. The big fucking bar weighs a pound."

"Anything else?"

"I'd like my dick sucked by the warden's hot secretary."

"I'm afraid you'll have to settle for the chocolate."

"Aim high and settle, right?"

"Sure. So about Brian Cosby?"

"What was your question?"

"My firm is looking for him," I said. "You once helped him find a safe house. Any ideas where he might go to hide?"

"Haven't seen the dude is something like five years," Maples said. "Did you know if you eat enough chocolate at one sitting you can actually get a euphoric high?"

"Where did you hide Cosby?" I asked.

"Who remembers? Could have been anywhere. Wait. I think it was this house in Jersey," Maples said. "Yeah, Jersey. Some people I knew had this house by the shore. They used it mostly as a place to get high. I ran into Brian in I think it was Yonkers and he was all strung out looking for a place to crash. That's got to be it."

"How long ago was this?"

"When did they have the hurricane that wrecked the shore?"

"Four years ago."

"That long ago, huh?"

"So it was before the hurricane of 2012 then?"

"Yeah, but … wait, what month did the hurricane hit?"

"October, third week," I said.

"It was summer," Maples said. "I remember because I ran into him at the race track where they have flea markets now instead of races. It's a good place to rip stuff off, but only in the summer."

"See him after that?" I asked.

Maples shook his head. "Course I been in here for the last three years."

"Sure."

"My guess is if the cops can't find him he's dead," Maples said. "Junkies tend to have short life spans you know."

"I know."

"Anything else?"

"Nope."

"I counted five questions," Maples said.

"Five chocolate bars will be sent to your cell."

"The big fuckers," Maples said. "None of that one ounce shit."

*****

"From five years to four," Hawkins said.

"Four years is still a long time," I said. "For all we know Cosby could have been killed in Hurricane Sandy."

"When are you talking to what's his name?"

"Coopersmith. Tomorrow. I don't have my hopes up it will produce anything," I said. "I might go down to Florida and talk to Cosby's parents."

"Do you want me to call them and set it up or spring yourself on them as a surprise?" Hawkins asked.

"Definitely a surprise," I said. "Any progress on the list of names."

"Maybe tomorrow," Hawkins said.

I stood from the chair and reached for the phone on the desk.

"Help yourself," Hawkins said.

I called Ellen's number and her machine picked up. "Ellen, it's Kellerman," I said. "I have a question I need to ask. I'll call you back later when you're home from work."

I hung up and looked at Hawkins.

"I'll call the prison in Pennsylvania and tell them you're coming," he said.

"I'll stop in tomorrow when I return," I said.

*****

By late afternoon, I was giving the heavy bag a going over at Roth's gym. A kid in his twenties, a heavyweight of about my height approached me and said, "Hey, pops, old Roth said you might be willing to spar with me a few rounds."

I looked at the kid.

"Forget it," I said.

"I'll take it easy on you, pops. Don't worry."

"I'm not worried, I said.

"Roth said you could fight," the kid said.

"I can," I said. "Doesn't mean I will."

The kid walked away shaking his head.

I returned to the heavy bag. A minute or so later, Roth showed up.

"The kid wants to be a fighter," he said.

"I gathered. Is he any good?"

"Naw. His old man is a cardio whatever … a heart doctor," Roth said. "He asked me for a favor. If I could convince the kid to quit the idea of fighting and return to college."

"Go convince him then," I said.

"Some people don't hear words," Roth said. "They gotta be shown."

I looked across the gym to the ring where the kid was shadow boxing.

"One round," I said.

"That's all it should take," Roth said.

We walked to the ring where Roth said, "Hey, kid, it's your lucky day. Kellerman agreed to spar with you."

The kid grinned at me.

"I'll take it easy on you, pops," he said.

"Sure you will, kid," Roth said as he put a glove on my left hand. "Sure you will."

Once both gloves were on, I climbed into the ring.

"Hey, he's not wearing headgear," the kid said.

"Don't worry about it," Roth said. "You wanted to spar, spar."

The kid looked at me.

"Pops is waiting," I said.

The kid was on the balls of his feet and started dancing around me and when he tossed a soft left jab, I went underneath and unleashed a right uppercut that caught him flush on the jaw and set him to the canvas and out.

I looked at Roth.

"Okay?"

"A regular fucking Picasso," Roth said.

*****

From Johnny's office I used his phone to reserve a roundtrip flight to Philadelphia and rent a car. Then I tried Ellen again.

She was home.

"Hello Mr. Kellerman," she said. "I got your message a little while ago."

"Couple of things," I said. "Cosby was seen as recently as four years ago by Maples. The other is what can you tell me about Cosby's parents?"

"Not a lot really," Ellen said. "I know that Mr. Cosby was an investment banker on Wall Street and was pretty well off. He retired about ten years ago and they moved to Florida. I know they tried their best to help Brian, but it didn't take."

"Any idea where in Florida?"

"Hold on."

Ellen was gone about a minute and said, "Boca Raton," when she returned.

"Any address?"

"No. I never got the address from Brian; I don't think he knew it. Just a phone number," Ellen said.

"Let me have it," I said.

She read off the number and I scribbled it down on a slip of paper.

"Thanks. I'm going to see Coopersmith tomorrow and then I'll see if I can find Cosby's parents," I said. "What are you doing Wednesday night?"

"Not a thing. Why?"

"I might have something new to report," I said. "Know what a block party is?"

"Yes."

"Come after work," I said. "I'll hold a spot for you in the lot next to my car. Use the Eighth Avenue entrance."

"Okay," Ellen said.

"Good."

After hanging up, I checked with information and found the number invalid. The Cosby's did have a number, but it was unlisted.

I left Johnny's office and went to the bar.

He set me up with a mug of coffee and a shot of bourbon for himself. It was too late to hit the library to use a computer and Johnny didn't have one.

But Cindy did. A laptop. She let me borrow it and signed into it at the bar. I used both websites I belong to and conducted a search on the Cosby's.

Bradford Cosby's age was listed at sixty-one. He retired young, probably to get his wife away from their son. A thorough search produced an address in Boca Raton.

Elizabeth Cosby died six years ago at age fifty-four.

I used Google Earth to zoom in on the Cosby residence in Boca Raton. It was a large house on the beach. Big backyard, three-car garage, a private walkway to the ocean.

I looked at my watch and then asked Johnny for the phone. He gave me the wireless and I called Hawkins at home.

"Couple of things you can do for me tomorrow," I said when he picked up.

"Go ahead."

"The Cosby's have a beach house in Boca Raton with an unlisted number. See if you can get it," I said. "And Elizabeth Cosby, Brian's mother passed away five years ago. See if you can find a cause of death."

"I'll see what I can do," Hawkins said.

"I'll swing by tomorrow afternoon sometime," I said.

I handed Johnny the phone.

"And here I thought you wouldn't have to work this hard for the money," he said.

"Set up the board," I said. "I feel I can beat you tonight."

Forty-nine moves later, I toppled my king and went home.

Chapter Fourteen

"I've been in here almost four fucking years," Coopersmith said. "I neither care nor know where Brian Cosby is then or now. In short, I don't give a shit."

"Did the warden tell you why I'm interested in him?" I asked.

"He has a kid. So what? My mother had a kid. So did yours."

The table we sat at wasn't very wide. Coopersmith was cuffed to the iron ring.

"You don't want a kid to have the opportunity for a better life?" I said.

"My trust fund doesn't stop because I'm in here," Coopersmith said. "In two years, when I get out, I'll have three hundred thousand waiting for me in one lump. And I'm going to shoot every fucking nickel of it into my veins."

I reached under the table and grabbed Coopersmith by the balls and yanked on them.

"Hey what …?" he said.

I squeezed really hard and he shut up and doubled over with his face on the table.

"Do you give a shit now?" I said.

I looked at the two guards at the door and apparently they were too busy watching the floor to notice.

"You want to cooperate with me, don't you?" I said and squeezed harder.

"Please," Coopersmith whimpered with tears in his eyes and snot running from his nose.

"What happened to the tough guy?" I said and pulled on his balls. "Where did the little girl come from?"

Coopersmith started to blubber and cry.

I released my grip.

"Catch your breath," I said. "We'll start over."

It took about five minutes before Coopersmith regained enough composure to continue.

"Brian Cosby, tell me what you know," I said.

"He disappeared," Coopersmith said. "That's all I know."

"When?"

"Maybe a year before I was sent up."

"Any idea why?"

"Junkies come and go," Coopersmith said. "Who keeps track?"

"Last time you saw him was where?"

"Lemme think," Coopersmith said.

I lit a cigarette. "Take your time."

"When was that hurricane that wiped out the Jersey shore?"

"Four years ago."

"I thought it was longer than that."

"Time flies."

"It had to be right around then," Coopersmith said. "There is ... was a crack house on the beach I used to hangout in sometimes. I was there ... no ... he was already there when I showed up. Yeah, he was already there."

"How did he seem?"

"How did ... what's that mean? Seem?"

"Did he appear anxious or scared? Did he give you the impression he was trying to hide from something or somebody?"

"You don't know shit about junkies," Coopersmith said. "Anxious, scared and hiding is a way of life for us."

"Look asshole, wise off to me one more time and I'm going to beat you to death right in front of the guards and they won't lift a finger to help you," I said. "Know why? Because to them you're no better than dog shit on the bottom of their shoe. Now, last time, did he say anything out of the ordinary besides the usual junkie chatter?"

Coopersmith stared at me for a few moments. Then I saw something click in his eyes. "I can tell you something," he said. "What's it worth to you?"

"What do you want?"

"A hundred dollars worth of candy."

"No problem."

"That storm was like in October, right? I remember we were freezing there by the ocean in a building with no heat," Coopersmith said. "I remember Cosby said something like he was going south to get away from the winter, something like that."

"Did he say where down south?"

"No, but he said he had people who would take him in."

"That wasn't so hard now, was it," I said.

"Don't forget the candy," Coopersmith said. "It's the least you can do for the case of sore balls."

"I doubt they were getting much use anyway," I said.

*****

On the way home, I stopped off to see Hawkins in his office.

"I got the number for the Cosby's," Hawkins said. "I spoke with Mr. Cosby at length. At first he was hostile at just the mention of his son, but when I explained the situation about his grandson, he cooled down. He's agreed to see you. I told him to expect your call."

"What about his wife, how did she die?" I asked.

"Apparent suicide," Hawkins said. "Drug overdose. That's all he would disclose."

"I'll call him and head down on Friday," I said.

"How did it go with Coopersmith?"

"Saw Cosby right before the hurricane of 2012," I said. "In some flophouse on the Jersey shore. He said that Cosby planned to go south before the winter."

"Interesting," Hawkins. "Why Friday, why not sooner?"

"I have to go to a block party," I said.

"A what?"

"Never mind," I said. "What about the list of fake names?"

"Should have something tomorrow."

"I'll talk to you tomorrow."

*****

It was raining when I parked the car in the lot and entered the Bar and Grill.

Johnny was behind the bar and set up a mug of coffee when I took a stool.

"You have visitors," he said.

I turned and looked at the booth against the wall where Maria and Denise were seated. I stood up and took my coffee to the booth.

"We're not stalking you if that's what you think," Maria said.

"It's a public bar," I said.

"Can you sit for a minute?" Maria asked.

They were seated opposite each other and I chose to sit next to Denise so I could look at Maria.

Each had a half full glass of white wine.

"I'm selling the house," Maria said. "Denise's mother is a real estate agent and feels confident I can get as much as four hundred and fifty thousand or in that range."

"It's your house," I said

"That's what I wanted to talk to you about," Maria said. "Documents show you paid the remaining eighty-seven thousand on the mortgage while I was away."

"I did so willingly and without your permission," I said. "You don't owe me a thing if that's what you're thinking."

"Eighty-seven-thousand is a lot of money," Maria said.

"I didn't say it wasn't," I said. "I said you don't owe me a thing."

"You don't make it easy," Maria said.

"There's nothing to make," I said. "It's your house. Sell it if you want to. The money is yours. I make no claims to any of it."

"I told you he'd be a prick about it," Denise said.

I turned to her. "Open your mouth again and I'll close it for you," I said.

Denise looked at Maria. "He'd hit a woman?"

"Oh yeah," Maria said. "Kellerman is an equal opportunity thug."

"Is there anything else?" I said. "I have things to do."

Maria looked at Denise. "Can you wait in the car? I'll only be a minute."

Denise nodded. I stood and she scooted past me and went to the door. I sat.

"I still love you as much as I always did," Maria said.

"I told you once, I don't share," I said.

"Even if you never saw her again? It would be like she didn't exist."

"I'm not alternate side of the street parking," I said. "Monday, Wednesday, Saturday is my turn at the honey pot, she gets the rest. No thanks."

Maria took a small sip of wine. "Do you want to know where I'll be living?"

"Nope. It's not my business anymore."

"Well, that's plain enough," Maria said.

She stood up and walked out.

I took my coffee back to the bar.

"Feel like a game?" Johnny asked.

"No," I said.

Chapter Fifteen

"Mr. Hawkins told me to expect your call," Bradford Cosby said. "But I have to confess I've forgotten your name."

"Kellerman," I said.

"Kellerman. I won't forget again," Bradford said. "I also have to confess I was madder than a wet hen when Mr. Hawkins told me what his call was about. But when he explained how it would benefit my grandson I agreed to see you."

"If you can spare some time this Friday?" I said.

"I can," Bradford said.

"I expect to reach Boca Raton by noon," I said.

"I'll have lunch ready," Bradford said.

"Good. I'll see you then."

I hung up and returned the phone to Mrs. Parker.

"The block party is tonight," she said.

"I know."

"Will you be attending?"

"Johnny will skin me alive if I don't."

"I'll see you there."

After a quick change into sweats, I walked to the Y and worked out for ninety minutes. On the way back, the city planners and private carnival company were setting up in the streets.

I had time for a nap and slept for about ninety minutes. Maria haunted me in several dreams. She was still one of the most beautiful women I have ever encountered. In one dream, as I reached for her she kept moving backward. The more I reached, the more distance between us opened up.

I woke up briefly, fell back to sleep and had another dream. She was naked in my bed, but faceless. I kept trying to focus on her face, but the harder I tried the more of a blur it became.

The cats brought me to the surface by tugging on my hair. Their food bowl was empty and they were hungry.

I filled the bowl, changed the water, made some coffee and drank a cup with a smoke at the kitchen window.

It was amazing how quickly things came together in the street. Although it was just four in the afternoon and the block party wouldn't officially open until six when the grand marshal, Johnny Sanchez made a speech, hundreds were gathered on the sidewalks to watch the preparations.

After a quick shave and shower, I tossed on slacks, tee shirt and sports jacket and clipped the Browning .45 into the small of my back and went down to the Bar and Grill.

Johnny was in his office, preparing notes for his speech. For once he wore a tie with his suit, but I knew it would come off the moment he finished his introduction.

I used his phone to call Hawkins at home.

"Interestingly enough three names on the list of names Cosby may have used as an alias are real," he said. "All three are dead from an overdose. I'm checking to see if any of the three are actually Colby using the alias."

"Fellow junkies in arms," I said. "I spoke with Bradford Cosby. I'm flying down on Friday to see him."

"Good. I'll keep working on this list," Hawkins said. "Who knows what lurks beneath the rocks."

"I'll call you tomorrow."

I hung up and looked at Johnny.

"I hate speeches," he said.

*****

Johnny stood on a platform next to the priest from the Catholic Church located one block over and made his official block party kickoff speech. Lieutenant Sullivan and his six detectives stood in front of the platform at street level. When Johnny concluded, he turned the microphone over to the priest.

The Hell's Kitchen Block Party was spread out across three blocks. The first block had food venders on both sides of the street. Everything from cotton candy to sausage sandwiches to fried dough. The center block was reserved for gambling and games. The last block was all rides. Everything from the Ferris wheel to the Pirate Ship.

The event wasn't restricted to residents of Hell's Kitchen. People came from all over the City over the two day period the block party lasted. The event organizers and grand marshal, Johnny Sanchez, allocated all profits to various charities.

Sullivan's detectives did an hourly run to collect money from each vendor and take it to the church where it would be locked in a safe brought in just for the event. The safe had a drop slot on top and couldn't be opened by anybody except the event organizers and Johnny.

I crossed the street and made my way through a large crowd to the parking lot and waited by the Eight Avenue entrance.

Ellen was running late. Traffic was heavy and with Ninth Avenue closed for several blocks, it would be even worse.

At ten to seven, her Bronco turned into the lot. She spotted me and parked next to the Lincoln.

"I should have left earlier," she said. "I'm sorry for keeping you waiting. Traffic was a mess."

"I should have warned you," I said as I took her arm.

Only a few of the die-hard drinkers were in the bar. Cindy was tending as Johnny was still on the street somewhere.

"Grab a booth," I said. "I'll get us some coffee."

I went to the bar and Cindy filled two mugs and I carried them over to the booth Ellen chose by the window. I set the mugs down and sat opposite her.

"Couple of things," I said as I pulled out my smoked and lit one.

"Can you smoke in here?" Ellen asked. "I thought the City banned smoking in bars and public buildings."

"They did," I said.

Ellen grinned at me.

"I met with Coopersmith and he places Cosby at the Jersey shore right before Hurricane Sandy," I said.

Ellen took a sip from her mug and nodded. "We'd go there in the summer a few times. It's full of college kids with money and dealers on the beach looking to sell to them. They'd put undercover cops on the beach, but they're easy enough to spot. Pale as ghosts with hats to hide their earpieces and dark sunglasses and windbreakers to hide their guns."

"This was in October right before Hurricane Sandy," I said.

"Then Brian must have been desperate," Ellen said. "After Labor Day the beach is empty and it gets cold there pretty early."

"Would he use the beach as a place to hide?"

"If he was desperate enough, sure."

"Coopersmith said Cosby told him he was going south, that he had people there," I said.

"His parents?"

"I think so," I said. "His mother died four years ago."

"Elizabeth? How?"

"Drug overdose."

"That doesn't make … do you think Brian had anything to do with it?"

"I don't know. I'm meeting with Mr. Cosby on Friday," I said.

"Hard to believe one man could do so much damage," Ellen said.

"That list of names Cosby used as an alias, three of them are real and they are dead," I said. "He must have known them and used their names in a pinch. We're still checking the others."

Ellen sighed and looked out the window.

"Come on," I said. "I'll buy you a hot dog."

We stood and Ellen took my arm and we went out to the street.

"I would take your hand but you're so tall and I'm not," she joked.

We wandered around for a bit and settled for sausage sandwiches and fried dough and washed them down with cups of Cappuccino coffee.

I spotted a few of my tenants playing games and waiting for rides, but mostly they ignored me.

As we nudged our way through the block of vendors, Mrs. Parker caught up with me in front of an arts and crafts tent.

"Mr. Kellerman," she said as she eyed Ellen.

"Mrs. Parker, this is Ellen Fallen," I said.

"Hello," Ellen said.

"Hello, dear," Mrs. Parker said. "I haven't seen you before."

"I'd remember," Ellen said.

"Will I see more of you?" Mrs. Parker said.

"I don't … I'm not sure I understand," Ellen said.

"Mrs. Parker, I'll see you later," I said.

I steered Ellen toward the rides.

"What was that about?" Ellen said.

"Do you mind heights?" I asked.

"No."

"Good."

I bought two tickets to the Ferris wheel and we got on line.

"Who was that woman?" Ellen asked.

"She's my tenant," I said.

"Your tenant?"

"Get in," I said.

We got into a car and the attendant closed the bar locking us in.

When the wheel was fully loaded and we moved to the top, I pointed to my building. "I own that building," I said. "Mrs. Parker lives there."

"You own that building?" Ellen said. "Mr. Hawkins said there was more to you than met the eye."

"It's that way with most people," I said.

"That man Johnny Sanchez, is he a gangster?" Ellen asked as we went around and around.

"Johnny is a businessman," I said. "He's the chairman of this block party. All money goes to charity."

"I read somewhere that Al Capone gave money to little old ladies on the street," Ellen said. "That doesn't mean Capon wasn't a gangster."

We stopped at the top of the wheel. We were as high as a sixteen story building.

"Do you live alone?" Ellen asked.

"I have two cats," I said.

"Cats?"

"And no mice."

"Oh."

We slowly made our way to the bottom.

"How come you don't have a woman?" Ellen asked.

"Are you guessing or are you sure?" I said.

"Sure."

"Because?"

"Because you live alone with two cats."

We stepped out of the car and walked toward the food section.

"I had a woman for a very long time," I said.

"And?"

"It's over."

"Because?"

"She dumped me."

"Wow."

"For another woman," I said.

"Bigger wow."

"How about another Cappuccino?"

"Okay, but then I have to go," Ellen said. "I'd like to make the meeting at Saint Paul's."

We made our way through the crowds to the Coffee Clutch cart and I ordered two Cappuccinos. There was no place to sit so I took Ellen's arm and guided her to my building where we sat on the steps.

"I guess nobody can tell you to move," Ellen said.

"One of the benefits of being the landlord," I said.

I lit a smoke and watched the crowds.

"Do you think there's a chance you'll find my son?" Ellen asked.

"I don't know," I said. "I'll tell you when I feel it's hopeless."

"Well, you've already gotten further than the FBI and police," Ellen said.

"What happens to the four hundred thousand if your son can't be located?" I asked.

"I don't know," Ellen said. "There is a second will in case of that event. It can't be read until all avenues have been explored."

"Who determines that?"

"The attorney holding the will. It has to be proven to him that all evidence and documentation showing every effort has been made to find my son has failed."

"We have a long way to go before I give up," I said.

"Mr. Hawkins said you were a bulldog," Ellen said.

"What time is your meeting?"

"Ten."

"I'll walk you to your car," I said.

We left the empty cups on the steps and stood up. Ellen took my arm and we battled our way across the street.

At her Bronco, I released her am and she unlocked the door.

"I'll give you a full report on the meeting with Mr. Cosby when I return," I said.

"Do you cook?" Ellen asked.

"Not much," I said.

"Show up around seven," Ellen said and got behind the wheel.

After she drove off the lot, I found Johnny at a window booth in the bar.

He was sipping bourbon over ice.

I sat opposite him and lit a cigarette.

"Lieutenant Sullivan has just made the first drop," Johnny said.

"What time is the last?"

"After one in the morning," Johnny said. "That's the last drop."

"Who's Sullivan's boss?"

"Captain Larkin," Johnny said. "I've already spoken with him."

"And?"

"He hates dirty cops."

"I'll see you later then," I said.

"I saw you walking around with Miss Fallen," Johnny said. "She's a pretty girl."

"Yeah, but you're a little too old for her," I said.

*****

I woke from a quick nap around ten in the evening. I smoked a cigarette at the window and watched the crowds for a while. The block party was in full swing. Lights from the vendors and rides lit up the streets.

The cats watched from the window ledge, thoroughly engrossed by the lights, sounds and crowd.

I took a steaming hot shower and dressed in black jeans with a matching tee-shirt and black walking shoes.

Not that I needed it, but I tossed on a black windbreaker when I left the apartment.

I wandered around the street for a bit and grabbed another Cappuccino and sat on my steps to drink it. I lit a smoke and tuned out the party for a few minutes and thought about Brian Cosby.

The closest I placed him so far is a sighting four years ago.

A great deal can happen in four years. Cosby could and probably was dead. As he was the quickest and surest route to Ellen's son, I was hoping for alive.

I didn't notice the building superintendent Rafael until he emerged from the alleyway and sat next to me.

"Mr. Kellerman," he said. "Enjoying the fair?"

"I'm enjoying the Cappuccino," I said. "The rest is a pain in the ass."

"Can I ask you something?" Rafael said.

"Sure."

"I need a raise. I work a second job as a doorman at the Carlton ten at night to six in the morning four nights a week to pay for my son's tuition," Rafael said.

"Where does he go?" I asked.

"Boy's Academy on West 68th."

"Expensive school," I said.

"Three hundred a month tuition, plus uniforms and books."

"Did you speak to Mrs. Parker?"

"I did. She said you need to approve it."

"You do a good job around here," I said. "I'll talk to her and tell her to give you a raise."

"Thank you," Rafael said. "It means a lot."

"Education is important," I said.

Rafael stood up. "Well, the garbage isn't going to load itself."

I nodded. That's the thing about garbage; it needs to be taken out.

The party was to officially end at midnight and I walked down to the church and went around back to the service door that was open. I went in and followed the hallway to the vestments changing room behind the altar.

Johnny, Police Captain Larkin and the priest were standing at the door that led to the altar, looking through the window in the door at the altar.

I joined them and glanced through the small window. The only light inside the church came from candles. Candles in long stem holders in the center aisle and dozens and dozens at the altar.

"You're Kellerman?" Larkin said.

I nodded.

"Sullivan is as tough a nut as they come," Larkin said. "And as dirty a cop as I've ever seen."

I looked at the priest.

"This is a house of God," the priest said.

"As I recall, Father, Jesus had a hissy fit in the temple at the money changers," I said.

The priest looked at me and sighed.

"Father, why don't you have a glass of wine?" Johnny said.

"I believe I will," the priest said.

The room was pretty airtight and I lit a cigarette.

"You can't smoke in a church," Larkin said.

I nodded to the priest. He was standing beside the table where the wine is stored, drinking a glass and puffing on a butt.

"Kellerman," Johnny said, softly.

I looked through the window. Sullivan had entered the church and was walking up the center aisle. A large, canvas money sack was in his hands. He walked past the heavy safe and turned left and opened the door to a confessional booth.

I removed my running shoes.

"Dear God, forgive the violence that is about to …" the priest said.

"Father, please," Johnny said.

I took a final hit off the cigarette and crushed it out in an ashtray on the wine table.

"Maybe you should go out back now, Father," I said to the priest.

He nodded and went to the back door.

I opened the door and stepped out to the altar. A quiet church amplifies every little noise into a loud echo, so I took it slow and easy in my stocking feet as I made my way to the confessional booth.

When I reached the booth Sullivan occupied, I could hear the rustling of cash through the door.

I grabbed the doorknob and yanked the door open. Sullivan was seated with a large pile of cash on the counter.

I gave him no chance to react. My hands went to his throat and I pulled him from the tiny booth and threw him to the marble floor. As he landed, I kicked him in the face. Before he could recover, I sat on his stomach and unleashed a dozen or more punches to his face.

He went limp.

He was done.

I stood up and looked at Johnny and Larkin who were now at the altar.

"His pockets are stuffed with money," I said. I looked at Larkin. "You might want to do something about that."

Larkin pulled his handcuffs and walked past me as I went up to the altar. I nodded to Johnny and returned to the vestments room for my jogging shoes.

The priest was out back, smoking another cigarette.

"You can go in now, Father," I said.

*****

"He had slightly more than twenty thousand stuffed into his pockets," Johnny said.

We were in the Bar and Grill. It was closed. Cindy was wiping glasses at the bar.

"The priest said to tell you he will say a prayer for you at mass tomorrow," Johnny said.

I lit a cigarette.

"I think I'm going to get some sleep," I said.

Outside, everything was locked up tight. Six private security guards patrolled the locked tents and rides.

The cats were asleep on the bed and I joined them.

Chapter Sixteen

After a ninety minute workout at the Y, I showered at home and dressed casually in slacks and a pullover shirt.

I left the apartment and walked to Fifth Avenue to the giant bookstore and browsed for a while and finally selected a dozen books for Davis and paid to have them shipped to the prison.

The Bar and Grill was serving lunch by the time I returned and I had a plate of roast beef with mashed potatoes and gravy.

For once Johnny joined me and ate at a window booth.

Afterward, we played a marathon game of chess that went seventy-three moves. On the sixtieth move, I thought I had him, but Johnny skillfully backed me into a corner and I toppled my king when he had me in checkmate.

"By the way, Captain Larkin has agreed to act as courier to the church tonight," Johnny said.

"Am I being relieved from my duties as watchman?" I said.

"I don't think it's necessary after last night, do you?"

"Nope."

"Okay to use the phone?"

"Be my guest."

I used the phone at the bar and called Hawkins.

"Located another two names on the list," Hawkins said. "One dead, the other doing time in Glades in Florida."

"What's his name?" I asked.

"Barry Camden."

"Doing time for?"

"It's a laundry list," Hawkins said. "Shall I call the warden?"

"Yes, but make the appointment for Saturday," I said. "I'll stay over an extra day."

"Expense money running low?"

"Barely dented it."

"Call me later after I speak with the warden."

I hung up and returned to the booth.

"I'll be gone for a few days," I said. "Florida."

"Watch the sun," Johnny said. "It's scorching down there this time of year and you Irish burn so easily."

*****

I packed an overnight bag with enough clothes to last three days in a pinch. Then I went down the hall to use Mrs. Parker's phone.

"I was just wondering about you," Ellen said when she answered my call. "If you left for Florida yet."

"Early morning flight tomorrow," I said. "I'll be stopping by Glades prison to see a Barry Camden, another name off your list. What can you tell me about him?"

"I never met him," Ellen said. "It's a name Brian used sometimes when he checked us into a motel and sometimes to forge checks. Brian had a checkbook with Camden's name on it."

"Okay, thanks," I said. "I'll see you when I return."

"Don't forget dinner."

"Seven sharp," I said.

"I'll see you then."

I returned the phone to Mrs. Parker.

"Two things," I said. "First is I have a quick business trip to make. I'll be back late Saturday. Do you have the new key for my apartment?"

"I took the liberty of having an extra made when the locksmith was here."

"Good. The second is I want you to give Rafael a raise."

"How much?"

"Work it out with him," I said. "He works a second job as a doorman for Christ sake."

"Early flight?"

"Seven in the morning."

"Are you going down to the block party?"

"Wasn't planning on it."

"Feel like some beef stew and a movie?"

"No RomCom's," I said.

"I was thinking some Charles Bronson," Mrs. Parker said.

"How about I pick up some dessert from the party?"

"Italian pastry would be nice."

I left the apartment and went down to the block party. I got a box of assorted Italian pastry and brought it back to Mrs. Parker's apartment.

We ate beef stew and watched a Charles Bronson classic called Hard Time, a film about illegal street fighting during the depression. After dinner, we ate pastries with coffee and out of nowhere, Mrs. Parker started to cry.

"What is it?" I asked.

"Oh, I'm just an old fool of a woman," she said as she grabbed a tissue and wiped her eyes.

"Why do you say that?"

"Today is my son's birthday," Mrs. Parker said. "I called him and asked if he could pick me up so I could spend the day with him and my grandchildren. He said they had plans and couldn't come to the City."

She started to cry again and I stood helplessly by and waited for her to stop.

When she went dry and wiped her tears with another tissue, she went to the bedroom and returned with a large shopping bag.

"I went to Bloomingdale's and got him these gifts," she said. "It's not every day a man turns fifty."

"No, no it isn't," I said. "Mrs. Parker, there's still a half box of pastry left. Would you care to watch another movie with me?"

"Why, yes I would Mr. Kellerman," she said.

Chapter Seventeen

My plane landed in Fort Lauderdale at ten forty-five and, as I had just the small carry-on bag, I skirted past baggage claim and went right to the car rental counter.

I rented a sedan with a GPS unit. After grabbing a large coffee, I entered the address for Cosby's oceanside home and left the airport.

The forty minute drive took over an hour as the GPS doesn't take into account the tons of road construction I encountered along the way.

The Cosby home overlooked blue ocean. The house was in the million plus range with a large lawn and flowers in front, a cul-de-sac driveway and three-car-garage.

Bradford Cosby answered the door himself when I rang the bell. He was around six-feet-tall, with silver hair, brown eyes and wore glasses. He was dressed casually in chinos and polo shirt.

"Mr. Kellerman?" he said.

I showed him my license and glanced at it and said, "You're not what I expected."

"I get that a lot," I said.

"We can talk on the deck until lunch is ready," Cosby said.

I followed Cosby through a beautifully furnished living room to the sliding glass doors that led to the backyard deck. The deck wrapped around to the left side of the house and overlooked the ocean. There was a wood staircase from the deck to the beach that must have had two hundred steps in it.

There was a large patio table with chairs, a massive barbeque grill and a wood bench that ran the width of the deck.

"Coffee, tea or soft drink," Cosby said. "I gave up alcohol after … Elizabeth died."

"Coffee is fine," I said.

"Be right back. Make yourself comfortable."

I grabbed a seat at the table while Cosby returned to the kitchen. He returned a few minutes later with a tray that held a carafe, mugs, cream and sugar. He poured and then took a seat.

"Where to begin?" he said.

"Mr. Hawkins explained to you that your grandson stands to inherit four hundred thousand dollars left by Mr. Fallen?" I said.

Cosby nodded. "We spoke at length."

"Start anywhere you like," I said. "I'll ask questions as we go along."

Cosby took a sip of coffee and said, "How do you keep them down on the farm once they've been to Paris? Are you familiar with that song?"

"I've heard it," I said. I sampled the coffee. It was expensive and damn good.

"Brian started using drugs when he was just fifteen," Cosby said. "He was in a private academy on Staten Island where all the kids came from money. It's not hard to find drugs when you have the means. He was expelled during his junior year and that was the first time he went to rehab. Obviously, it didn't take."

"It rarely does the first time," I said.

"Or the second, third or sixth," Cosby said. "His last stint in rehab, Brian turned eighteen and after that, he took off. You can imagine how this wore on his mother. Brian would show up from time-to-time when he needed money or clothing. After a while, when I realized our son was lost, I stopped giving him money."

Cosby paused to sip some coffee.

"I made the decision to relocate to Florida when Brian showed up one night demanding money and I refused," Cosby said. "In front of Elizabeth, he put a knife to my throat and demanded money. I gave it to him just to get rid of him. Elizabeth had a breakdown and that's when I decided to retire from the firm and get her as far away from him as I thought possible."

I sipped coffee and waited.

"We didn't see him for years," Cosby said. "Elizabeth became very depressed. Brian is our only son and you can imagine how a mother would feel. She began seeing a psychiatrist twice a week and it helped greatly. She started to live again. We became active in various charities and events and she even took up ballroom dancing. Then out of the blue Brian showed up four years ago in early November. He was broke, strung out and desperate for money. I refused and called 911. He ran and the police didn't find him. A few nights later, he broke into the house while I was attending a charity function for the Boca Police Department and beat up his mother. He stole cash, her jewelry, some paintings and silverware. She recovered from the physical beating but not the mental. She took and entire bottle of sleeping pills before I went to bed and when I found her, it was too late."

I heard a noise and looked down the staircase at a woman who was walking up.

"I'll get to that in a moment," Cosby said. "After Elizabeth's death, I contemplated suicide myself. There just didn't seem to be any reason to exist anymore. However, on the advice of my doctor, I began attending workshop groups for parents with kids hooked on drugs. There I met Claire. She was a widow with an adult son in similar circumstances as Brian. We've been married two years now."

Clair came onto the deck. She was an attractive brunette in her late fifties. She was dressed casually in tan slacks, white shirt and whisper thin sweater.

"Clair, this is Mr. Kellerman," Cosby said. "He is from the lawyer I spoke to on the phone."

We shook hands. "Hello," she said. "I hope you are hungry. Lunch is keeping warm in the oven."

Claire baked a chicken parm to die for and we ate at the patio table. Cosby extended the retractable awning to provide shade and we continued talking well into coffee and dessert.

"It's been four years now since I've last seen Brian," Cosby said. "I don't even know if he's still alive. Drug addicts rarely make it to forty I'm told."

"More coffee?" Claire asked after she cleared the table.

"Yes, thank you," I said.

Claire filled my mug, and then went into the kitchen.

"Mr. Cosby, do you believe Brian murdered Mrs. Fallen and kidnapped the baby?" I asked.

"I do," Cosby said. "I've seen what he can do when desperate for a fix."

"Have you had any contact with Brian by phone or through the mail since you last saw him?" I asked.

"No."

"What do you do these days, Mr. Cosby?" I asked.

"I've gotten back in the game so to speak," Cosby said. "After Claire and I were married almost two years ago, I set up an office in the house. I mostly manage my money, buy and sell stocks and make small investments."

"I'm glad," I said.

"As for the baby, I have no doubt Brian sold it on the black market," Cosby said. "I seriously doubt he'll ever be located."

"I'm not ready to throw in the towel just yet," I said.

"If there's anything I can do, please ask. The boy is after all, my grandson," Cosby said.

"I'll do that," I said.

"Actually, is you do manage to locate the boy, I will match Mr. Fallen's amount that he left in his will," Cosby said.

"You're very generous."

"Like I said, he's my grandson too."

"Well, I won't take up anymore of your time," I said.

"Are you staying in town?"

"Actually I'll be driving down to Miami-Dade," I said.

Cosby and Claire walked me to the door.

"Mr. Kellerman," Claire said at the door. "Many years ago, after my son beat me up for drug money, I took the advice of the police and bought a gun and learned how to use it. If Brian comes around and tries to hurt us, I won't hesitate to use it."

*****

I drove south to Miami-Dade County to the hotel I reserved a room for the night. It was a five minute drive from the Everglades Correctional Institution.

The hotel had a decent enough gym and after I checked into my room on the sixteenth floor, I changed and went down to the gym located on the fourth floor. There were several Stairmasters, some weights and Smith Machines. Between everything I managed a decent enough ninety minute workout.

Back in my room, I showered and changed and then ventured out for a walk around town. Technically the prison was located inside Miami, but not the place people think about from the old Miami Vice television show. It was all private homes with pink roofs, palm trees and coconuts, parks and golf courses.

I had the address of the prison and decided to walk to it. I found it on SW 187th Avenue. The facility was enormous with high fences and armed guards in watch towers. And even palm trees.

The return trip to my hotel took about twenty minutes.

The hot afternoon sun soaked me though my shirt. The hotel had two pools, one outdoor. I didn't have a bathing suit, but the lobby gift shop sold them and I picked up a pair.

I changed in my room and took the elevator to the outside pool. Six or seven people were soaking up the sun; a few were in the pool.

I'm not much for lazing around poolside, but I had much to think about and digest and it was as good a place as any to get it done.

I wasn't close to calling it quits on locating Brian Cosby, but the trail was room temperature and unless Barry Camden dropped a bombshell in my lap tomorrow, I didn't foresee a reincarnation anytime soon.

The five o'clock sun was brutal with temperatures in the low nineties. I decided to take a dip in the pool, but the water was so hot it actually made me sweat even more. I switched out to the indoor pool where the air conditioning was cranked way up.

I grabbed a lounge chair and mulled things over for a while. Brian Cosby hadn't been seen by anybody I contacted in four years. The boy was now ten-years-old, so no one even knew what he looked like. With the matching grant, eight-hundred-thousand-dollars were at stake. Life-changing money for a boy's future.

Brian Cosby was smart. Wanted for murder and kidnapping, he evaded the FBI for a decade. You don't do that without being smart. He stayed under the radar, used aliases, bought his dope from small time dealers and avoided people he knew.

He didn't just live under the radar he fell completely off the grid.

I quit thinking and returned to my room, took a shower and decided to order dinner from room service. I ordered a steak with pie and coffee for dessert and watched a crappy movie on HBO for a while.

Afterward, I sprawled out on the bed and worked the situation around in my mind for a while until my eyes grew heavy.

*****

Barry Camden was serving eighteen months for passing bad checks and classified as a medium security risk. Arrested for possession of stolen property and drugs, he copped a plea, gave up his dealer and was given the reduced sentence.

He was in his early forties, but looked sixty. Hawkish and thin, he was missing most of his front teeth and spoke with a lisp because of that.

"I been in here six months now," Camden said. "They got this rehab program here and I'm the cleanest I been in twenty years. I even exercise some and jog around the track. The prison dentist is making me teeth and as you can see I could use them."

"I'm happy for you," I said. "What can you tell me about Brian Cosby?"

Camden looked at me.

"What do you want for the conversation?" I said.

"I got a sister," Camden said. "Lives in Fort Lauderdale. She has four kids and her husband died a year ago in a car accident. Can you send her some money to help her out?"

"I can arrange that," I said.

"Give me your word."

"You have it."

"And your business card," Camden said. "If she doesn't get the money in a week, I'm calling you up on phone day."

I dug out my wallet and gave him one of Hawkins's business cards. He tucked it away into his shirt pocket.

"Brian Cosby is one motherfucker," Camden said. "Did you know he killed a woman and almost killed his own parents? Kidnapped his own kid, too. That's when he killed the kid's mother."

"I did know that," I said. "Tell me what I don't know."

"How much you sending my sister?"

"Depends on what you tell me that's new."

"Last time I saw him was in Daytona about two years ago," Camden said. "That place is heroin heaven come spring break. We hung out for a bit and he started bragging about how he has this new source of income. So I says, I says, yeah Brian, what's that?"

"And he said?"

"He says he set up this sweet deal," Camden said. "He said he was blackmailing this lawyer who sold his kid. He said 'why didn't I think of that sooner' and laughed his fool head off. I asked how much and he said a grand a month. At five bucks a pop, that keeps you high all month. And then some."

"Did he say how he gets the money or who the lawyer is?" I asked.

Camden shook his head. "He likes to brag, but goes only so far."

"And that was in Daytona two years ago?"

"It was early fall, so not quite two years."

"Have you had any contact or heard from him since them?"

"You mean like a letter or phone call?" Camden said. "We're junkies, man, if it ain't in front of our face it's out of mind. The primary focus of a junkie is getting high and staying high. Everything else is peripheral."

"Can you remember how he looked?" I asked.

"Looked?"

"Yes, looked. Can you describe him as he looked two years ago?"

"Lemme think," Camden said. "He's a tall guy, but hunched over a bit from when I first knew him. His hair was thinning, but that happens to all junkies because we starve ourselves of nutrition. Teeth were yellowing, so I wouldn't be surprised if some have fallen out by now."

"Do you know where he scored his dope?"

"H is as easy to score as a box of Milk Duds," Camden said. "He could find it anywhere he goes and he goes a lot. All junkies move around to stay ahead of the game."

"Okay," I said. "Thanks for your time."

"My sister?"

"What's her address?" I said. "Five thousand will be in the mail by tomorrow."

"Well hell, if I knew you was going to be so generous I would have made some shit up to along with the truth," Camden said.

"Sometimes the truth is worth more," I said.

Chapter Eighteen

"He's a slick son of a bitch, I'll give him that," Hawkins said.

We were at his conference table. There was a pot of coffee and two mugs. He filled the mugs and I took a sip from mine and then lit a cigarette.

"Do you have to?" Hawkins asked.

I blew a smoke ring. "Question is, who is the lawyer being blackmailed?"

"How the hell … let me find you an ashtray," Hawkins said.

He went to his desk, rummaged around and returned with a candy dish and set it on the table.

"Let's talk this out," I said and flicked ashes into the candy dish.

"He burned through the money he got for selling his kid on the black market," I said. "He dried up his source of ready money with his parents and now he's desperate for cash."

Hawkins said. "So he dreams up the perfect scam. Blackmail the lawyer that sold his baby on the black-market. The lawyer has no choice but to pay or risk prison himself."

"Question is, who is the lawyer?" I said.

"Do you have any idea how many lawyers there are in New York City?" Hawkins said. "Not to mention the metro surrounding areas."

"How many specialize in adoption?" I asked.

Hawkins looked at me.

"Find out," I said.

"I suppose I can contact the American Academy of Adoption Attorneys," Hawkins said. "But there are also Social Services to consider."

"I doubt Social Services is in the habit of selling babies on the black market," I said.

"When I speak to the Academy, should I include Jersey and Connecticut?" Hawkins asked.

"Yes, but it's doubtful Cosby went outside the metro area," I said. "He snatched the kid from the Fallen home and ditched it fast. That means he made the deal before hand. The lawyer and buyer were already arranged before he broke into the Fallen home, killed Mrs. Fallen and took the kid."

"I agree," Hawkins said. "But say I compile a manageable list of attorneys, do you think the guilty one is simply going to admit their guilt for the asking."

I crushed out the butt in the candy dish and lit another cigarette. "Ellen Fallen said you described me as a thug," I said.

"Hey, that was just a …" Hawkins said.

"It's okay, Cal," I said. "It's accurate. You're a lawyer. Do your job. When you have the list, I'm a thug, I'll do mine."

Hawkins looked at me. "Heaven help me the company I keep," he said.

*****

After I left Hawkins, I drove north and stopped into the bookstore on Fifth Avenue and purchased a chess set and had it shipped to Davis. I included a box of one hundred envelopes and writing paper and a book of one hundred stamps. I wrote a short note. *You make the first move.*

*****

Ellen answered her door wearing designer jeans, a designer sweatshirt and white socks. Her hair was down and there was a touch of makeup that added a glow to her cheeks and accented her eyes.

"Talk first, then eat? Eat first, then talk?" she asked.

"Put on some coffee," I said.

We talked in the backyard at the patio table. I smoked, Ellen listened and we went through an entire pot of coffee.

"Nothing that cold-hearted bastard does surprises me," Ellen said when I wrapped it up. "He plotted to kidnap my son and sell him to the highest bidder. Somehow that seems worse than a desperate junkie making a spur of the moment decision."

I watched slight mist form in her eyes.

"Well, I promised you dinner," she said.

"Forget cooking," I said. "Let's go out for a bite."

We made it to my car and the floodgates opened. Ellen placed her hands over her eyes and cried a deep sighing cry that lasted for many minutes. The jag ended when she ran out of tears and gulped air and dry-heaved.

"While I was going through hell in the prison hospital, he was plotting to kidnap my son and sell him," Ellen said when she regained enough composure to speak. "That means going in he knew he would have to kill one or both of my parents."

"Want to forget about going out?" I said.

"I need to go to a meeting," Ellen said. "I can drive myself."

I started the engine and said, "Where to?"

*****

Saturday night was a big night for AA meetings. The basement of the nearby Baptist Church had forty chairs set up and it was standing room only.

We stood in back and listened to several tales of woe until the meeting ended with a prayer.

"Want to grab some takeout on the way back?" I asked when we were on the return trip.

"I could use a pizza," Ellen said. "A really fattening pizza with everything on it and dripping with grease."

She knew this pizzeria that used brick ovens and we grabbed a large to go with a side of garlic rolls and a two-liter bottle of Coke.

We ate in the backyard under the stars. It was a clean, warm evening with just a hint of breeze.

"So, how sorry do you feel for me right now?" she asked when we were done eating.

"I have a policy," I said. "I never feel sorry for anybody. Whatever happens it's called life. Feeling sorry never accomplished anything except to hold you back."

"Can I ask you for a really big favor?"

"Ask."

"If I'm alone right now, I'm going to drive to the nearest liquor store and buy a bottle and get ripping drunk," Ellen said.

"Do you have a washer and drier?" I said.

"Of course."

"Good. I'll need something clean for the morning."

*****

We watched a movie on some cable channel and shared a bowl of popcorn. Somewhere between the time the alien invader saved the earth or destroyed it, I'm not sure which; Ellen was sound asleep with her head on my shoulder.

She had changed into light green pajamas and I didn't know what else to do with her, so I lifted her in my arms and carried her to her bedroom. She woke up briefly and put her arms around my neck, but was sound asleep again when I tucked her into bed.

I watched another movie after that, a western I'd never seen before and then I slept on the sofa. It was an eight-foot-long sofa and wide and comfortable and I didn't stir until light from the living room window hit me in the eyes.

I checked on Ellen and she was still asleep. I put on a pot of coffee and drank a cup in the backyard and smoked a cigarette.

After a while, still in her pajamas and holding a mug, Ellen came out and joined me at her patio table.

"I bet when you took this job you didn't know it included babysitter," she said.

"How are you at making breakfast?" I asked.

"Pretty good actually."

"Think you can whip something up while I grab a shower?"

Ellen nodded. "Your clean clothes are still in the drier."

"Give me ten minutes then," I said.

"You can use the shower in my bedroom or the one in what used to be my parents room," Ellen said.

I went in, grabbed my stuff from the drier and took a shower in the other bedroom. When I returned to the kitchen, Ellen was making breakfast at the oven.

Bacon was sizzling in a pan. Home fries were in a second pan, toast was in the toaster and Ellen asked, "How do you like your eggs?"

"Any way is fine," I said.

Ellen scrambled a dozen eggs of which I got the lion's share. We ate in the backyard at the table under a warm morning sun.

"Thank you for staying last night," Ellen said. "You really are a very nice man for a thug."

"I have my moments," I said.

"So what next?"

"We'll see if we can find the lawyer Cosby is blackmailing," I said. "The last time Camden saw Cosby was two years ago. A lot can happen in two years."

"That's what you said about six years," Ellen said.

"Just don't want you to get your hopes up too high," I said.

Ellen nodded. "I won't."

"I best head back," I said.

"I'll walk you to your car."

I tossed the overnight bag on the front seat and got behind the wheel.

"Hey Kellerman, thank you for being a gentleman," Ellen said.

"I might be a thug, but I wasn't raised in a barn," I said.

Ellen grinned.

She was still grinning as I backed out of the driveway and drove away.

Chapter Nineteen

The cats were in the kitchen window and were completely indifferent to me when I entered the apartment.

Mrs. Parker kept their food and water bowls full and the litter box clean, so they had very little use for me in general.

I changed into sweats and left the apartment and jogged over to the Y. I usually take Sunday off from working out, but the plane ride, sleeping on a sofa and large breakfast had me feeling lethargic.

I ran twenty-five laps on the track to loosen up, then hit the weight room for about an hour and ended with another twenty-five laps on the track.

After the second shower of the day, I tossed on a pair of jeans, a tee-shirt and socks and went to see Mrs. Parker.

"They give you any problems while I was away?" I asked.

"Heavens, no. I did take a liberty. I picked up a catnip plant at the pet store and left it on top of your refrigerator," Mrs. Parker said. "They can eat the leaves whole."

"Thank you," I said. "I never though of a catnip plant."

"I'm going to eat at the Pub tonight," I said. "Maybe you'd like to join me?"

"Across the street?"

"Seven-thirty. I'll pick you up. Okay?"

"Alright."

*****

"You'll be happy to know the block party did record business this year," Johnny said. "Mostly because the cops didn't get to steal anything."

"So Captain Larkin owes you a favor," I said.

"Don't go there," Johnny said.

"Even if it means the possible arrest of the decade?" I said.

Johnny stared at me across his desk.

"I'll mention it," he said. "If he agrees to listen, you explain it to him."

"I'll be back at seven-thirty for dinner," I said. "With Mrs. Parker."

"The old woman from your building?"

"She's my building manager," I said. "It was her birthday the other day and I thought I'd bring her over for the heartburn."

"Say no more," Johnny said.

*****

The cats, occupied at the kitchen window didn't even notice my entering the apartment, and if they did they didn't care. They were in attack mode and made tiny chirping noises and if the gate on the window wasn't there, they would have pounced on a bird that landed on the fire escape.

I took the catnip plant down from the top of the refrigerator and picked off two leaves. I found that if you rub the leaves they release and oil that smells like mint.

The cats picked up the scent, jumped down from the window ledge and began meowing against my legs.

"Sure, now you notice me," I said.

I gave each a leaf and they swallowed it whole and wanted more. I gave each another three leaves, then replaced the plant on the refrigerator.

The catnip kicked in and they went crazy for about ten minutes, chasing each other around the apartment, rolling on the floor and acting like kittens.

Then came the crash and both cats went to my bed, curled into balls and took a nap. I decided to join them for a bit and slept for about an hour. When I woke, I had time for a quick shower and change of clothes and then went down to Mrs. Parker's apartment and knocked on her door.

She let me in as she wasn't quite ready. I stayed in the living room and studied the photographs of her son and his family that were on the walls and tables. He was a large, burly kind of man with black hair and dark eyes.

"I'm ready Mr. Kellerman," Mrs. Parker announced as she entered the living room.

"I know you've told me, but I forget your son's name," I said.

"David."

"Right. He works for the city, doesn't he?"

"Sanitation Department for twenty seven years. He's a route supervision on Queens Boulevard."

"Right. Well, let's go."

*****

The bar was packed, but Johnny kept a booth open by the window. The Yankees were playing The Mets in The Bronx and a good crowd at the bar was following the game.

Johnny was behind the bar, Cindy and another waitress worked the tables.

"I had no idea this place was so popular," Mrs. Parker said as we took seats at the booth.

"Sunday night is always like this," I said.

Cindy went behind the bar and Johnny came to the booth.

"May I join you?" he asked.

"You're Mr. Sanchez?" Mrs. Parker said.

"And you are Mrs. Parker," Johnny said.

"I am and if you're going to sit, then sit," Mrs. Parker said.

Johnny sat.

We ate a massive meal of chicken parm with spaghetti with garlic rolls on the side. Mrs. Parker drank white wine, Johnny his bourbon while I stuck with Coke with lemon.

Mrs. Parker told stories of her days working for the phone company back in the fifties, the death of her husband and how she came to live in the Kitchen. She was born just a few blocks from my building and moved to Queens in the sixties when she and her husband purchased a home in a neighborhood called Rego Park. After her husband died twenty years ago, she gave the house to her son, who was renting an apartment in Flushing.

Johnny told some stories I had never heard before about growing up in a rough neighborhood in Puerto Rico in the fifties and sixties before his family moved to The Bronx.

We had chocolate ice cream cake with coffee for dessert.

It was after eleven when I walked Mrs. Parker back to the building.

At her door, she said, "I know that you're being nice to me because you feel sorry for an old woman, but thank you."

"You're a good neighbor, Mrs. Parker," I said. "It has nothing to do with feeling sorry."

I sat around the apartment for a while and thought about Brian Cosby. It takes a certain type of scumbag to do the things that he did, but there was no shortage of scumbags in the city.

Or anywhere else for that matter.

The soldiers Davis and I killed in Iraq for raping Kurd women where scumbags. So was Mrs. Parker's son. So were millions of others just walking around going through their daily scumbag lives.

The adoption lawyers who sold babies to desperate couples took scumbag to a new level.

If I were to find Ellen's son and get to Brian Cosby, it would take an act of God and a great deal of luck.

And maybe a scumbag or two along the way.

Chapter Twenty

I followed the white station wagon along Queens Boulevard as the driver, David Parker, made his rounds.

I had no idea what a Sanitation Department Supervisor did, but it appeared that he followed garbage trucks around and observed as they picked up trash on their routes.

Shortly after noon, the station wagon pulled into the parking lot of a diner in a neighborhood called Hillside. I parked a few spots from him and watched as David Parker entered the diner.

I followed him into the diner where he went to the men's room. He was alone at a urinal when I came in and locked the door.

I waited until he had zipped up and then I cut him off as he walked to a sink. He was a big, beefy man with the looks of a bully.

"David Parker?" I said.

"Who are …?"

I kicked him in the balls and he collapsed at my feet.

"I'm your mother's landlord," I said. "And you don't want to see me when I'm angry and not calm like now."

David held his balls and rolled around on the floor.

"Are you listening to me, David?" I said. "Say yes or I'll kick your balls into your fucking throat."

"Yes," he rasped.

"Okay, good. Now going forward, you and your family are going to visit with your mother at least twice a week on Sunday. Is that clear? Say yes."

"Yes."

"You're going to bring her flowers and candy and take her to dinner. Yes?"

"Yes."

"You're going to make her last few remaining years happy ones. Yes?"

"Yes."

"If I find you aren't doing these things by this Sunday, I will make your wife an early widow," I said.

I pulled out the Browning .45 and stuck it against David's balls.

"Do you believe me?" I said.

"Yes."

I put the Browning away.

"Have a nice lunch," I said.

*****

"Twenty-five adoption lawyers just in the city," Hawkins said. "Over a hundred and fifty in the state. Add in Connecticut and New Jersey and the total is over four hundred."

We were at the conference table in his office. We had mugs of coffee and I lit a cigarette.

"Do you have to … oh, never mind," Hawkins said as he went for the candy dish.

He set the dish in front of me and sat. "It could take years to investigate a list that long," he said.

"I think you can shorten the list by removing any lawyers that weren't practicing ten years ago," I said.

Hawkins nodded.

"Then we look at complaints filed at the Bar Association and see who may appear less than desirable," I said. "Then we look at who was disbarred for dubious practice and maybe spent some time in prison."

"Is this the favor that could get me disbarred?" Hawkins asked.

"Not if we have a police captain on our side," I said.

"Anyone I know?"

"You'll find out if he agrees to join the team."

"Oh, we're a team now?"

"You brought this to me," I said.

Hawkins sighed. "When will you know if he's with us and should I continue the research or hold until he is or isn't?"

"You managed three questions in one sentence," I said.

"I am an attorney after all," Hawkins said.

"Continue, but tread lightly," I said. "If it's something you need to ask a cop, put it aside."

I crushed out the butt in the candy dish and stood up. "I'll call you as soon as I talk to the police," I said. "If you come across something urgent, get a hold of me through Johnny."

"The company I keep," Hawkins said.

*****

Around eleven o'clock in the evening, I watched the Bar and Grill from my bedroom window. I was in the dark so I couldn't be seen from the street. I drank coffee and cupped my hand so I could smoke a cigarette.

After a catnip induced frenzy ended in a crash, the cats were entwined on the bed, sound asleep.

At eleven-thirty a black sedan pulled up to the Bar and Grill and parked beside a hydrant. It was too dark to see the face of the man that got out and entered the bar, but I knew it was Captain Larkin.

Ten minutes later, Cindy came out, stood on the sidewalk and looked up at my window. She held the pose for about a minute, and then went back inside.

I tossed on a sports jacket and left the apartment.

Cindy was behind the bar when I entered and walked straight to Johnny's office. I knocked once and opened the door.

Johnny was behind his desk. Larkin in a chair. Each had a glass of bourbon.

"I'm normally not in the business of doing favors, but under the circumstances I can make an exception," Larkin said.

"Are you a precinct captain or from headquarters?" I asked.

"Precinct," Larkin said.

"Maybe we can get you promoted," I said.

"And maybe you better explain yourself," Larkin said.

"My client is a recovering addict," I said. "Ten years ago, while she was serving time, her six-month-old son was kidnapped from her parent's home and her mother was murdered. The FBI and police believe it was the baby's father, Brian Cosby, also a junkie, who did the kidnapping and murder. He was never found and the case went as cold as Whitey Bulger.

"Staten Island, right?" Larkin said. "I remember."

"The baby's mother has recovered and is living the straight and narrow," I said. "A few months ago, her father passed away and left the boy four hundred thousand in a trust fund. The boy's mother doesn't want her son back. After ten years it wouldn't do the boy any good to open that can of worms. She just wants to give him the trust fund as her father willed."

"No contact, just deliver the trust fund?"

"That's what I was hired to do," I said. "The client doesn't even want to know where the boy is."

"Shouldn't you take this to the FBI?" Larkin said.

"The FBI doesn't do local murder cases and since a ransom demand never came forward, the case has been shelved," I said. "NYPD has no statutes of limitations on a murder case, correct?"

"And I fit in how?" Larkin asked.

"Cosby would have had to get rid of the kid quickly," I said. "He had to have a contact already in place to take and sell the baby on the black market. Who better to sell a baby on the black market than an adoption attorney?"

I could see the gears turning in Larkin's mind. He finished his drink and Johnny poured him another.

"The lawyer I'm working with has compiled a list of adoption attorneys in the tri-state area," I said. "You could save us a great deal of trouble by doing background checks on them and weeding out the good ones from the rotten apples. Right now, Cosby is blackmailing this attorney for his drug money. The attorney may be ripe for the picking. We get the attorney, we also get a murderer and possible the location of the boy. The boy gets his inheritance and you get credit for solving a decade old murder and kidnapping case that the FBI couldn't."

"And you get?" Larkin asked.

"I'm being paid," I said. "That's all I get and want. The credit is yours. If it gets you a seat at One Police Plaza, congratulations."

"What about Social Services?"

"Falls into your area of weeding out," I said. "Although I doubt Cosby had contacts inside their department."

"Who is your attorney and when can I meet him?" Larkin asked.

"Got a private number?"

"My cell phone."

"I'll call you tomorrow," I said.

"You did me a solid with Sullivan, Kellerman," Larkin said. "IAD is all over my precinct and they're not done yet, so there may be some more rotten eggs to dispose of. That said, you be straight with me and I'll be straight with you. Fuck me and you'll live to regret it. Do we understand each other?"

"We understood each other before I even walked in here," I said.

"Good."

"I'll call you tomorrow," I said.

Larkin removed a business card from his pocket and handed it to me.

"Do you have a car?" he said.

"I do."

"If we have to drive anywhere, we'll take your car," Larkin said. "Everybody in the department knows mine."

"No problem."

Larkin finished his drink.

"Goodnight gentlemen," he said.

After Larkin left, Johnny said, "How about a game?"

Chapter Twenty-one

Larkin arrived at Hawkins's office just as the receptionist brought in a fresh pot of coffee with three cups.

"I'm Cal Hawkins," Hawkins said as he shook hands with Larkin.

Larkin looked at me.

"How is it the FBI and local police couldn't make a dent in this case and you've gotten this far working alone?" he said.

"Time has added evidence," I said. "And they have rules to follow. I don't."

Hawkins guided us to the conference table where he had stacks of folders at the ready.

"I've only gone back ten years as that's our timeframe," Hawkins said. "We're interested in adoption attorneys with complaints against them for unethical practices and attorneys with revoked licenses. Inside the same timeframe, we'd like a look at anybody at Social Services fired and or arrested for unethical practices. I realize the FBI and local PD might have done the same ten years ago, but like Kellerman said, time has added evidence and they've quit looking."

Larkin looked at the folders. "I need copies."

"These are yours," Hawkins said. "I have copies for myself."

"This won't be an overnight deal," Larkin said.

"It's been ten years," Hawkins said. "Nobody expects overnight."

Larkin looked at me. "Did you drive?"

"I did."

"Let's put all this in a box. You can give me a ride," Larkin said. "I took the subway."

*****

"Had lunch?" I said.

"No."

"Pick a place, I'll buy," I said.

"Know the Tribecca Diner?"

"I do."

"Best chili in the city," Larkin said. "Park at a hydrant. I have a police sticker I can leave in the window."

*****

Larkin was correct about the chili, it was pretty damn good.

"I did some homework on you," Larkin said.

"I expected," I said.

"United States Marine with a sealed file," Larkin said. "Black Ops, Special Forces or none of my business?"

"A squad was assigned to protect Kurdish oil wells," I said. "A buddy and I stumbled across five US Soldiers raping some Kurdish women. We shot and killed them and spent a year in the brig while the Pentagon figured out how to deal with it without embarrassing the military. They finally decided to bury the entire incident, discharged us and sealed the files."

Larkin stared at me.

"I'd tell you to verify the story, but you can't," I said.

"You've had a PI license for twelve years, but no office and not even a phone number," Larkin said.

"I like peace and quiet," I said. "I only work directly for lawyers, so there's no need of an office and phones are a nuisance."

"Is Sanchez a friend or associate?"

"It's possible to be both," I said.

"Johnny Sanchez is called the Godfather of Hell's Kitchen," Larkin said. "What does that make you?"

"Johnny doesn't fuck people and neither do I," I said. "This case is exactly what it appears to be. And so am I."

Larkin nodded and then ate some chili. "I've been passed over for Deputy Inspector five times," he said. "And each time I was passed over the promotion went to a captain in homicide."

I ate some chili.

"After twenty-five years on the job, a cop has just two basic goals," Larkin said. "To live long enough to collect his pension and to not fuck up badly enough to lose that pension."

"How's the dessert in this place?" I asked.

*****

I burned off lunch with a ninety minute workout at the Y and jogged home through rush hour clogged streets.

It was one of those hot afternoons where the air was absolutely rancid and could use a good rain to wash away the stench. None was forthcoming however and I had to settle for a shower once I was back in the apartment.

I hadn't planned on going out again for the rest of the day. I fed the cats some catnip and played with them for a while until they bottomed out and crashed on the bed.

I went to the bedroom window, lit a smoke and thought about the odds of actually finding Ellen's son. It was doubtful at this point that finding Brian Cody would lead to the boy. Finding the lawyer that sold the boy was more the route to take going forward.

The lawyer could tell us who he sold the baby to ten years ago.

I tossed on a warm-up suite and went down the hall to borrow Mrs. Parker's phone.

"Kellerman, I was just thing about you," Ellen said.

"Will you be home tonight?" I said.

"Let me check my social calendar," she joked. "Yes."

"Okay if I stop by?" I have a few things to report."

"Sure. Want dinner?"

"We'll order out. My treat."

"In that case, I won't dress up," Ellen said.

Chapter Twenty-two

We sat on the living room sofa. Ellen wore black jeans, a short-sleeve white tee-shirt and white socks. Her blonde hair was down past her shoulders. She wore no makeup, but she didn't really need any. Her blue eyes without makeup seemed a deeper blue, almost marble-like in quality.

She had set out coffee pot, cups and ashtray when I arrived. I sampled the coffee and then lit a smoke.

"Busy day at work," Ellen said. "I missed lunch, so I'm starved."

"Order up a storm then," I said.

"There's a Thai place on Piedmont Avenue that's really good," Ellen said.

"Sure."

Ellen used her cell phone to call the restaurant and ordered half the dinner menu.

"So what few things did you want to report?" she asked me after she hung up.

"Some progress reports and a question," I said. "I'll start with the progress. Hawkins and I feel the only way we're going to find you son is through the person that Cosby sold him to. In all likelihood a dishonest adoption attorney. We can only take it so far without outside help. We don't have any evidence to take it to a judge for warrants to search financial records, phone taps and things like that. A police caption with an eye on a promotion owes me a favor and he's agreed to dig deeper than Hawkins or I can. If the lawyer is paying Cosby blackmail as seems to be the case, we'll need a judge to open financial records. The police captain can do that for us. Understand?"

Watching me, Ellen nodded.

"And your question?" she said, softly.

"It's a tough one, but it needs to be asked," I said.

Ellen nodded slightly. "Ask."

"Is it possible while you were in prison those first six months that your parents could have contacted an attorney to put the baby up for adoption?" I said.

Ellen stared at me.

"They were in their fifties at the time and …"

Ellen lashed out with her right hand and slapped me across the left cheek. Her tiny hand packed a wallop and the slap stung.

"...may not have wanted to raise a child with a daughter facing seven years," I said.

She slapped me again and this time it really stung.

"Is it possible?" I said.

The question was followed by a third slap.

"Is it possible?" I said again.

Ellen balled her tiny hands into fists and came at me, punching. Her fists struck me in the mouth, the nose and chest. She punched until she was exhausted and leaned forward with her face in her hands.

"Is it possible?" I said.

"Oh, fuck you," Ellen said.

"Is it possible?" I said.

"Get out of my house," Ellen said.

"Is it possible?" I said.

Ellen looked at me with tears in her eyes. "Yes, it's fucking possible," she shouted, stood and rushed off to the kitchen.

I sat for a minute, tasting my own blood in my mouth. There was a handkerchief in a back pocket and I used it to dab at my mouth and nose.

Then I stood and went to the kitchen. Ellen was in the backyard at the patio table. I slid open the doors and stepped outside and took a seat next to her.

"It's possible," she said.

"Did you father keep a lot of old papers, correspondence, and things like that?"

"There are crates of stuff in the garage."

"We need to go through them."

Ellen nodded.

"We lived together for three years after I came home," she said. "The subject never came up once."

"Parents are like cats in a way," I said. "They are very good at masking their pain."

Ellen grinned. "Is that some Eastern philosophy thing?"

"Nope, an observation from a cat owner," I said.

Ellen turned and looked at me. In the dim light from the floodlight, I mush have looked a mess.

Ellen gasped and said, "Did I do that?"

"I'm not one for scourging," I said.

"Come in the kitchen," she said and took my hand.

We entered the kitchen and Ellen said, "Take a chair at the table," and went to the bedroom.

She returned with a bottle of hydrogen peroxide, a bag of cotton balls and a wash cloth. "I don't have any rubbing alcohol, so I use this," she said. "Take off your shirt."

I removed my shirt while Ellen filled a bowl with warm water.

"Honest to God, why didn't you stop me?" she asked as she carried the bowl to the table.

"You needed to vent," I said.

Ellen wet the cloth and gently wiped blood from my face. "Vent maybe, but a Rocky movie no," she said.

"A few lumps never killed anybody," I said.

"Hold still," Ellen said. "This stuff hurts."

She poured some hydrogen peroxide onto a cotton ball and dabbed at my cuts.

"Ouch," I said.

"Told ya. Hold still."

She dabbed some more.

"That stings," I said.

"Don't be such a baby," Ellen said.

The front doorbell rang.

"I'll get it, my treat," I said as I stood and grabbed my shirt.

"That hardly seems fair," Ellen said. "A beat down for a free dinner."

"It's your expense money," I said.

I went to the door where a Thai deliveryman handed me two shopping bags and a bill for seventy-seven dollars. I gave him a hundred dollar bill and told him to keep the change.

"Inside or out?" Ellen asked when I toted the bags to the kitchen.

"Out."

She carried plates, silverware, cups and a large bottle of Coke to the patio table. I carried the bags and she dished out the food.

"Wait," Ellen said and dashed inside. The floodlight went out and she returned with two lit candles in stick holders and set them on the table.

"The floodlight attracts bugs," she said.

Hungry, I dug into the food. Thai is similar to Chinese, but the spices are deeper, richer and more flavorful.

"So what exactly will we be looking for?" Ellen asked.

"Correspondence of some kind," I said. "A letter from Social Services. A notice from an adoption attorney. Something like that. Cosby needed a starting point. He just didn't pull a crooked adoption attorney out of his hat."

Ellen exhaled loudly. "This is going to take a while," she said.

"A while we got," I said.

We finished eating and Ellen showed me the garage. There were thirteen cardboard carton stacked against the back wall. Each carton contained two letters of the alphabet.

"I haven't packed up my father's den and his desk yet," Ellen said.

"Well, we'll get an early start in the morning," I said. "I'll be here by seven and you can take off for work."

"You can stay over and sleep in the guest room," Ellen suggested. "I have some time off coming to me; I might as well use it."

"Got an extra toothbrush?"

"Several."

"I need to make a call," I said.

I used the phone in the kitchen and called Mrs. Parker.

"Mr. Kellerman, you won't believe it," she said with joy in her voice. "My son called and he and his family are taking me to brunch this Sunday."

"That's wonderful, Mrs. Parker," I said.

"Yes. I take it by your call you want me to watch the cats?"

"Check them tonight and tomorrow," I said.

"No problem."

"Maybe if I'm around Sunday, I can meet your son?"

"That would be lovely."

"Good night."

I hung up and looked at Ellen.

"The old woman from the block party," she said.

I nodded.

"I'll show you the guest room," Ellen said.

It was smaller than Ellen's room, with a full size bed and a small bathroom.

"There's an unused toothbrush in the medicine cabinet, but no mouthwash," Ellen said. "Mouthwash contains alcohol."

"No problem," I said.

"Well, I guess I'll turn in," Ellen said.

After Ellen left, I stripped down to tee-shirt and shorts and brushed my teeth with the new toothbrush. I inspected my face in the mirror. A few minor cuts, a couple of welts, a swollen lower lip, no big deal.

The bed was comfortable enough and after a while I started to drift off to sleep.

*****

I'm a light sleeper. The slightest noise and my eyes are open. It's a habit leftover from my days in the Corps.

I heard a noise in the bedroom and was instantly awake. Ellen was standing over the bed. The room was dark except for a hint of light coming from the tiny nightlight in the bathroom.

A long tee-shirt ended at her knees.

"Is something wrong?" I asked.

Ellen flipped down the sheet and got into bed beside me.

"Keep your morning wood in your shorts, this isn't a sex thing," she said. "I'm feeling a bit afraid and could use a friend."

"Sure," I said.

"Turn."

I turned onto my right side.

Ellen put her face into the back of my neck and slung her arm over my chest.

"What are you afraid of?" I asked.

"The same thing as everybody else," she said. "Fear of the unknown."

Chapter Twenty-three

While Ellen cooked breakfast, I carried the first two boxes marked A and B and C and D into the living room.

I found a pair of old sweatpants and a tee-shirt that fit me in the guest room closet and I wore those while my clothes were in the washing machine.

Ellen made French Toast with sausage patties and we ate in the backyard in the cool of the morning.

"I suppose you think I'm silly being afraid of the dark," Ellen said.

"Everybody is afraid of something," I said.

"Even you?"

"Even me."

"What is the big bad Kellerman afraid of?"

"Growing old. Not being able to do the things I can do now."

"Not dying?"

"Being old and useless is worse than dying," I said.

"Maybe you're right about that one," Ellen said.

"Let's get to work," I said.

*****

I took A and B, Ellen went with C and D.

"Pull out anything from ten years ago that might pertain to your son or even yourself," I said. "We'll read everything later."

It took most of the morning to empty the four boxes and we found not a single document that even mentioned the baby. Most papers were client correspondence, insurance documents and documents concerning stock market investments.

Neither of us was hungry for lunch and took just coffee as we tackled boxes E, F, G and H.

From those boxes we found hospital reports on the condition of the baby at birth, police reports concerning Ellen's arrest and reports from Social Services.

"The baby was born in mid-April according to the birth records," I said. "The police reports are from a week later and Social Services in early April."

"Seems about right," Ellen said.

"It's after five," I said. "Tomorrow is Friday. We can pick this up again on Saturday if you want."

"It needs to be done," Ellen said.

"Okay. I'll be back first thing on Saturday."

I grabbed my clothes from the drier and changed.

At the door, Ellen looked at me.

"What?" I said.

She shook her head. "See you on Saturday."

*****

I used Johnny's office phone to touch base with Hawkins.

"You might actually find something in his old records," Hawkins said.

"Have you heard from Larkin?"

"We touched base this morning," Hawkins said. "Nothing as yet."

"Once I've gone through all of Fallen's old files, I'll bring the findings to you and maybe we can put a meaning to them," I said.

"Call me when," Hawkins said.

I hung up and looked at Johnny. He was standing beside his file cabinet with a glass of his prized bourbon in his hand.

"What happened to your face?" he asked.

"I asked Ellen Fallen a question that needed to be asked and she didn't like it and beat me up," I said.

"This case is taking a very strange twist, don't you think?" Johnny said.

"They're all strange," I said. "Feel like a game?"

*****

I ate a plate of meatloaf with mashed potatoes and gravy while Johnny beat me once again at chess, although it took seventy-three moves before I surrounded my king.

In my apartment, I played with the cats after they ate some catnip leaves. When they crashed and burned, so did I.

When I tried to sleep, something nagged at me that I couldn't put a finger on. I did a review in my head to pass the time until I grew sleepy.

Two years is a long time to blackmail a lawyer without something happening. The lawyer could get fed up paying extortion money to a junkie and if he was connected enough, have the junkie killed.

If said lawyer was fed up enough and desperate enough, kill said junkie himself.

Said Junkie could have done the world a favor and overdosed and is no longer with us. He also, as happens with many junkies, could have been murdered.

Said junkie could have been arrested and is presently serving time, but if that were true he could be using an assumed name, although that possibility was remote.

There was another possibility. Brian Cosby could have found Jesus two years ago, cleaned up his act and was now living the quiet straight and narrow somewhere in small town America? Unlikely though.

Most probably, Brian Cosby was still blackmailing the lawyer for his drug money and living the life of a junkie on the run.

I went with that scenario.

Cosby would need a way to receive the blackmail money in a secure way every month.

Said lawyer would need a secure way to send money each and every month.

Checks and money orders were out. So were bank drafts. Sending cash was just plain stupid. Cosby and the lawyer could meet every month at a prearranged day and time, but that would mean Cosby would have to stick close or at least travel on a regular basis.

So if you want to send money to someone on a regular basis and do it under the radar and regardless of where the recipient was located, Western Union was a good choice.

There are thousands of outlets where you can walk in and send someone money simply by filling out some forms. On the receiving end, all you needed to do was show your ID and pick up the cash.

Even if the sender and receiver were using fake ID's, it wouldn't matter as long as ID's were presented and matched.

I needed to check, but I had no doubt the money transfer could be done on line, but I doubted a lawyer would agree to so easily traceable a transaction and I doubted even more that Cosby had a computer.

With the cats by my side, I finally drifted off to sleep.

*****

In the morning, I hit the gym at the Y hard for a ninety minute workout. An hour in the weight room and a hundred laps on the indoor track.

I walked home dripping wet. The eighty degree heat and sweltering humidity didn't help my condition and by the time I opened my apartment door, even my sneakers were water logged.

After a cool shower, I tossed on some clean sweats and went down the hall to use Mrs. Parker's phone.

Hawkins was in his office.

"Western Union," I said. "If I was being blackmailed and needed to send untraceable money to the blackmailer, Western Union is a good way to do it."

"It is, isn't it," Hawkins said.

"Call Larkin and run that by him," I said. "It's a long shot, but maybe he can get Western Union to do some leg work for us. See if like amounts are being wired every month on the same day and for how long."

"Larkin might be a mite testy when I call him," Hawkins said.

"Because?"

"He didn't think of it himself."

"I don't exist, remember," I said.

"Call me later."

When I returned the phone to Mrs. Parker, she was still excited about her son taking her to Sunday Brunch.

"Would you care to go with us?" she asked.

"I'll be away until Sunday night on business," I said.

"I'll watch the cats."

After I returned to my apartment, I changed in jeans, a pullover shirt and jogging shoes and went down to the coffee shop on West 57th Street for lunch. I read the sports pages in the newspaper while I ate.

When I returned home, I was surprised to see mail in my box. It was a letter from Davis. I went up to my apartment and opened it.

Pawn to queen one. You play black.

That's all the letter said.

I set up my chessboard on the coffee table. I moved the black pawn to queen one. Then I moved my white pawn to bishop one. I got out some writing paper and wrote that down and addressed an envelope to Davis at the prison.

I changed into clean sweats and dropped my letter in a mail box on the way down to Roth's Gym.

I put in ninety minutes worth of jumping rope, speed bag and heavy bag work and then sat with Roth to watch a pair of welterweights spar a few rounds.

"The kid wearing green has his first six rounder at the Brooklyn Armory next weekend," Roth said.

"He looks sharp. Crisp," I said.

"He's got the tools," Roth said. "I guess we'll find out if he's got the heart."

*****

"I never thought of Western Union," Johnny said. "I doubt Larkin did either."

I studied the chess board and then moved my knight.

"It will take some cooperation on Western Union's part," I said.

"Why wouldn't they cooperate?" Johnny said. "They've done nothing wrong."

Johnny moved his bishop across the board to block my knight.

"Neither did Apple."

I studied the board and planned five moves ahead and then backed my knight up.

"I know some people that could possibly expedite the process," Johnny said.

He attacked my knight with a bishop.

"How much?" I asked.

"Ten thousand," Johnny said. "He'll ask for fifteen, but he'll settle for ten."

"Set it up," I said.

I attacked Johnny's bishop with my queen.

"Stop by for a midnight snack," Johnny said.

He slid his queen across the board and captured my knight.

"Check," Johnny said.

I looked at the board.

"Goddammit," I said.

*****

After a quick nap, I grabbed a shower and was back in the bar a few minutes before midnight.

Johnny was at a booth. Cindy was pouring drinks. Johnny stood and I followed him to his office.

Seated in a chair opposite Johnny's desk, the round man wearing Coke bottle glasses and with a ponytail to his waist, stood up.

"Ira, this is Kellerman," Johnny said as he went to his desk and took the chair.

Ira looked up at me. His watery yes blinked behind his thick lenses.

"I need a simple hack job," I said. "Johnny tells me you can do that."

"I once hacked IBM for a Wall Street broker who wanted inside information," Ira said. "I once hacked the FBI for the Italian Mob so they could see what the feds were up to. I once hacked …"

"I get it," I said. "Can you do a simple job for me?"

"How simple?"

"I'm investigating a blackmail case," I said. "A man is paying the blackmailer every month for several years and I believe he's using Western Union to conduct wire transfers. Can you hack their records of transactions and find a payment to and from in like amounts over a two-year period?"

"You a cop?" Ira asked.

"Private Investigator."

"I'll do it only because you know Johnny," Ira said.

"How long will it take?"

"Not long. My fee is fifteen thousand."

"My budget is ten."

"Cash?"

"Of course," I said. "You deliver the results here and you'll be paid in full."

Ira looked at Johnny.

Johnny nodded.

"Monday night okay?"

"Fine," I said.

"Monday then," Ira said and left the office.

I looked at Johnny.

"It's amazing the people you know," I said.

"Isn't it," Johnny said.

Chapter Twenty-four

I parked the Lincoln in Ellen's driveway a few minutes after nine on Saturday morning. The morning started drab and overcast in Manhattan and was sweltering and raining in Staten Island.

Ellen answered the door wearing khaki shorts with a white tank top and white socks on her feet. Her hair was pinned up away from her neck.

"Not a good day for the air conditioning to break down," she said.

Two large fans were blowing in the living room.

"Where's the unit located?" I asked.

"Basement."

"Let's take a look."

The basement was surprisingly uncluttered. A large centralized unit was against the back wall with duct work leading upstairs. I checked the system and it didn't take long to figure out the problem.

"The compressor's burned out," I said.

"Can we call someone?"

"On Saturday that's overtime," I said.

"I don't care," Ellen said. "I can't stand this humidity."

"Got a phone book?"

Ellen called an emergency heating/air conditioning service and they said they could be there by noon.

At the kitchen table, with an oscillating fan blowing, Ellen drank iced tea while I stuck with regular coffee.

"I may have stumbled onto something," I said and told Ellen about my Western Union theory.

"I would have never ... yes, of course," Ellen said. "When I first met Brian and he was still on good terms with his parents they would often send him cash using Western Union."

I fired up a cigarette, thought for a moment and said, "Idiot."

"What?"

I stood up and grabbed the wall phone. "I need to make a quick call."

Cindy answered the phone and put Johnny on the phone.

"Can you get a hold of Ira?" I said.

"I can."

"Can you get his email address?"

"Probably."

"Hold on."

I turned to Ellen. "What's your email address?"

"It's ... oh, hand me the phone."

I gave her the phone and she recited the address, and then handed the phone back to me. "Tell Ira we'll be sending him a list of names Cody has used in the past for him to target as soon as he emails Ellen with his address."

"I'll tell him," Johnny said.

I hung up and looked at Ellen. "Let's get to work."

*****

We tackled boxes E and F and found several documents from Social Services and letters from the FBI and local police.

Around eleven o'clock, Ellen checked her laptop and said, "Got an email from someone with the address Warlord Emperor."

"Open it," I said.

She clicked on the email and said, "It says to call a phone number. Who is Warlord Emperor?"

"Ira, the hacker I told you about," I said. "I'll call him."

I used the kitchen phone and dialed Ira's number.

"Warlord," Ira said when he answered the phone.

"It's Kellerman," I said.

"Are you crazy?" Ira said. "Send a list by email? You never send a list by email. Email's can be hacked. I know. I hack them all the time."

"Take it easy, Ira," I said.

"It's Warlord Emperor and it will be an additional twenty-five hundred for the extra work," Ira said.

"Fine," I said. "Just do it."

"Read me the list of names," Ira said.

"Hold on," I said.

Ellen handed me her original list and I read each name off to Ira.

"Can you still make it Monday night?" I asked.

"No problem," Ira said and hung up.

"I know it's hot in here, but would you like something to eat?" Ellen asked. "I missed breakfast and I'm starved."

"Sure," I said.

I kept working in the living room while Ellen prepared something in the kitchen. I found several more FBI reports and copies of letters written by Ellen's father to the local police.

I just finished letter F when Ellen entered the living room.

"Lunch," she said.

We went to the kitchen where Ellen had prepared BLT sandwiches on thick, crusty slices of whole wheat bread and homemade French fries cooked in olive oil.

"My dad taught me how to cook," Ellen said. "He was quite good in that department."

We ate at the table. The BLT's were probably the best I've ever tasted. The fries were crunch, creamy and flavored with virgin olive oil and a hint of salt.

I just finished the last bit of my second sandwich when the doorbell rang.

"I'll show him the compressor," I said.

I took the repairman to the basement. He pulled apart the cover and did some tests.

"Compressor's gone," he said.

"Can you replace it?"

"Of course," he said. "Six hundred for the compressor plus four hours labor at ninety-eight an hour. It's Saturday, so that's time and a half."

I brought the repairman upstairs. He gave the quote to Ellen.

"Do it," she said.

The repairman left to pick up a new compressor. The rain had stopped and the sun came out causing the humidity to rise even higher. We worked boxes G and H from the sofa in front of the large oscillating fan.

Somewhere in the middle of box F, Ellen found a document and said, "Look."

I took the document. It was a Western Union wire transfer from her father to Ellen for two thousand dollars.

"Kansas City, eleven years ago," Ellen said.

I set the document on the pile and continued looking through the box. Ellen got up and returned to the kitchen.

I found a second wire transfer of money from her father to Ellen for twenty-five hundred sent just two months after the first, also in Kansas City.

I took it to the kitchen.

She was sitting on the table. Her stocking feet dangled six inches above the floor.

"I found another … what are you doing?" I said."

"Thinking."

"About?"

"Come here," Ellen said.

I walked closer to the table. Ellen's neck, shoulders and arms were covered in a layer of sweat.

"Closer," Ellen said. "I promise I won't bite or hit."

As I stepped closer, Ellen parted her legs and I stood between them. She locked eyes with me and didn't waver. She opened the top button of her shorts and slowly wiggled out of them and they and her panties fell to the floor.

I didn't move as she opened my belt, pants and slowly slid them and underwear to the floor.

Her hands found what they were looking for and her lips formed a tiny, Mona Lisa smile as I was already at full attention.

Still holding me with her right hand, Ellen placed her left hand behind my right leg and guided me slowly into her. She exhaled softly as we came together and still her eyes never left mine.

It felt as if I was covered in warm oil.

I moved a bit and Ellen placed both hands on my hips.

"Stay still for a moment," she said softly.

Then she closed her eyes and her head went back and her hips thrust against mine and after who knows how many seconds passed, she locked against me and her body shook and she all but exploded.

And so did I.

Ellen kept her eyes closed for a bit and when she opened them she smiled at me.

The doorbell rang and I stepped back and pulled up my pants.

"I'll be in the shower," Ellen said.

I went to the door and the repairman had a hand truck with a new compressor on it. "Gimme a hand getting this monster downstairs," he said.

We took the compressor down the steps and I left the repairman alone to his work. Then I went to Ellen's bedroom where her shorts, underwear and tee-shirt were on the floor and she was in the shower.

I removed everything and tossed it all on the bed. I slid the frosted glass door open and stepped into the tub.

The water was cool, refreshing.

Ellen looked up at me. I'm nearly a foot and a half taller and she had to stand on her tippy toes to kiss me.

"It's been so long I've almost forgotten what it's like," she said.

"Me, too," I said.

She gripped my arms and rubbed my biceps. "I find that hard to believe."

"It's true," I said. "Turn around."

Ellen turned. There were bottles of shampoo on the ledge and I grabbed one a put a healthy dab in her hair and worked it into a lather.

"The woman who dumped me for another woman, she was a cop at one time," I said. "She wasn't really guilty, but her department was dirty and she got caught up in the process. She was sentenced to two years and did eighteen months. I waited for her and didn't stray and when she got out, she waited two months to tell me she had gotten involved with another woman. Rinse."

I stepped away from the shower head so Ellen could turn and rinse off the shampoo.

"I can't reach your hair, but I can do your back," she said.

I turned and Ellen washed my back with a washcloth and soap.

"Can you," she said as her hands moved south, took me and began to gently stroke. "Do that again?"

I turned and my hands found her butt. It was smooth, round and firm.

Ellen grinned and continued to stroke me. "I guess you can," she said.

She guided me to a seated position with my back against the rim of the tub. Then she took the bottle of conditioner off the shelf, squeezed some on her fingers and applied it to herself.

She straddled my legs and lowered herself until we locked together. I looked at her breasts. They were perfection.

"Hold on," Ellen said and began to rock.

*****

"So is there anything left for her?" Ellen asked.

"Not on my end," I said.

We were at the backyard patio table. The sun had evaporated most of the water and the humidity had lowered a bit. Ellen drank iced tea. I had coffee and a cigarette.

"On her end?"

"Last I heard she was selling her house and probably setting up shop with her girlfriend," I said.

"I've been through to much shit in my life to be the other woman," Ellen said. "I can't and I won't."

"I know."

Ellen sipped some tea. "So what now?"

"I'll leave that up to you," I said.

"You can't do that," Ellen said. "I'm clean and sober a long time now, but I'm still an addict. Understand? An addict can become addicted to a person as easily as drugs or liquor. I don't want that. I can't have that. If there is anything between us it has to be us and not me. Me left alone is a disaster. Understand?"

"I think so," I said.

"A relationship is different than an addiction," Ellen said. "That's why I've stayed away from men since I left prison. But with you I couldn't help myself and now that we got the nasty out of the way, I'd like to know how you feel about it, about me."

"I'm a pretty simple guy really," I said. "I don't want or need much. I work when I want to and usually only when the work is worthwhile. I stuck by a woman for a lot of years who in the end didn't stick by me. That's life. I got over it. I wasn't looking for you and you weren't looking for me, but here we are and that's also life. So if you want to give us a try, I'm willing if you are."

"You'll be faithful to me?" Ellen said. "I won't tolerate a tomcat."

"Like a Boy Scout."

"I will be faithful to you like a Girl Scout, but without the cookies," Ellen said.

"Those peanut butter patties are pretty good," I said.

Ellen grinned. "You do know you're like a freaking giant, don't you?"

"My cats don't think so," I said.

The grin became a wide smile and Ellen's entire face lit up brightly. "I think it's time I met these cats of yours, don't you?"

"We'll finish up here tonight and head over to my place," I said.

"I have work on Monday," Ellen said.

"Take you back Sunday night," I said.

"Okay."

"The kitchen door slid open and the repairman stepped out. "Miss, I'm finished. The system is working fine now."

*****

Around seven, Ellen packed an overnight bag and I gathered up all the documents we had so far from her father's files.

I didn't feel like waiting an hour for the ferry, so I took the Verazzano to the Brooklyn Bridge into Manhattan.

"I try to make three meetings a week," Ellen said as I drove across the Verazzano. "I'd like you to go to one with me. Can you do that?"

"I can."

"I think it's important for me to know that you support me."

"Understood."

"Not much rattles you, does it?"

"No."

"So it doesn't bother you that as a girl I got taken in by a junkie con man, spent a third of my life as a junkie and sometimes hooker and gave birth to an addicted baby?" Ellen asked.

"If it bothered me I wouldn't be taking you to meet my cats," I said.

Ellen looked at me and then cracked up laughing. "I feel like I'm being taking home to meet your mother," she said.

"The cats would be harder to win over than my mother," I said.

"Meow," Ellen said.

*****

I parked in my spot, grabbed her overnight bag and as we crossed the street, Ellen said, "My God I'm starving."

"Eat in or out?"

"In. Definitely in."

"Ever had a real Cuban steak?"

"I don't think so."

"Have your cell phone?"

"I do."

"Good."

We reached my building. I let us in and we rode the elevator to the fourth floor. When I opened the door, the cats weren't in sight.

Ellen stood in the living room and said, "Where's all your ... stuff?"

"You're looking at it," I said.

The cats emerged from the bedroom and sat on the floor and looked at Ellen.

"They're beautiful. Siamese, right?"

"Brothers."

One, then the other approached Ellen and gave her the sniff test. To let her know she passed, the cats started to rub Ellen's ankles.

"You've been approved," I said. "Let me use your phone."

Ellen removed it from her bag. I called the Cuban restaurant on Ninth Avenue and ordered a feast. When I hung up, Ellen was on the sofa with the cats vying for her attention.

"So, living room, kitchen and bedroom," I said. "That's it. No phone, television, computer and sometimes, when it feels like it, the radio works."

"So this is what you meant by simple man?" Ellen said.

"More or less," I said. "I've learned to live with less which gives me time for more."

There was a knock on the door.

"Mr. Kellerman, is that you?" Mrs. Parker asked.

"It's me," I said. "I'm back early."

"Okay."

"Mrs. Parker?" Ellen asked.

I nodded. "Right down the hall."

One cat was on Ellen's lap, rubbing his head into her stomach. The other was perched on her shoulders, rubbing her neck.

"Do they ever stop?" Ellen asked.

I clapped my hands once and both cats jumped down and dashed into the bedroom.

I took her hand and walked Ellen to the bedroom where both cats were now on the bed.

"A king-size bed for one is a lot," Ellen said.

"The cats take up most of it," I said.

They were rolling around on the bed engaged in battle.

"So I see," Ellen said.

The doorbell rang. I went to the kitchen to buzz the deliveryman in and a few minutes later he was at the door with two large paper bags. I paid him and brought the bags to the kitchen.

"They're still fighting," Ellen said when she entered the kitchen.

"If they get too bad I have a water gun," I said.

I doled out the food. Cuban steaks seasoned and cooked to perfection, dirty rice with fried plantain, garlic bread and spicy custard for dessert. We gobbled it up in record time.

"I'm so full I don't think I can walk," Ellen said.

"You don't have to," I said.

I picked her up and held her in my arms. She didn't weigh more than a hundred and ten. I carried her to the bathroom and set her down beside the tub. I turned on the hot water and added Epsom salt, then put on the nightlight and turned off the lights.

Ellen looked up at me.

She wore a white sleeveless blouse with khaki shorts. I unbuttoned the blouse and slowly removed it and exposed a lacy white bra. I reached behind her back, opened the clasp and the bra fell away and Ellen's perfect breasts pointed up at me.

I reached behind her to mix cold with the hot and grabbed the bottle of scented oil left by Maria and added some to the water.

The shorts were held in place by an attached ribbon tied into a bow. I untied the bow, opened the hasp and zipper and the shorts fell to Ellen's ankles. The white underwear was frilly with lace stitched throughout.

I knelt down and lowered the panties to her ankles and removed both one leg at a time. Then I removed her socks and stood up.

"The drapes and carpet match," Ellen said softly.

"They do," I said.

I lifted her and gently lowered Ellen into the tub.

"Dunk under," I said.

She dunked under and when she came up, I grabbed a bottle of shampoo and squeezed some into hair. I worked the shampoo into a lather and rubbed her scalp for several minutes.

"Rinse," I said.

Ellen dunked under again to rinse off the suds.

I removed my shirt and wrapped my arms around her. "You're very good at this," Ellen said.

My right hand went under the water and found her opening and I used my finger to gently stroke her.

Ellen closed her eyes and rested her head against the rim of the tub. She sighed. "Very good at this," she said.

I kept massaging until she moaned and started to wiggle. Then I removed my pants and shorts and got into the tub opposite her.

"Don't spoil me, Kellerman," Ellen said. "I couldn't stand it if you broke my heart."

"The only thing I plan to break are some eggs in the morning," I said.

Ellen looked over and the cats were sitting, watching us.

"We're being watched," she said.

"Get used to that," I said.

*****

"Up, up, up, get off," Ellen said. "You're ripping me apart."

I rolled off her onto my back.

"I can't take your weight," Ellen said.

She rolled onto me and we locked into place. She leaned forward and put her right breast into my mouth.

"Hold on," she whispered. "We're going for a ride."

*****

We were close together on our right side. Both cats had settled in next to Ellen's stomach. She gently rubbed their ears and they purred like tiny motorboats.

"You'll find my son," Ellen said.

"I'll find him," I said.

"You promise?"

"I promise."

"Swear it."

"I swear that I will find your son."

"I believe you," Ellen said. "These cats are very loud."

"Yes, they are," I said.

Chapter Twenty-five

Sunday went by in a blink. We slept in and I made a large breakfast of omelets with peppers, a side of bacon and hash browns with coffee and OJ.

Around eleven o'clock, Mrs. Parker knocked on my door.

"My son is here to take me to brunch," she said. "I'd like you to meet him."

I went down the hall where David was waiting. I looked at him and extended my right hand. "Nice to meet you, David," I said.

He shook my hand and nodded.

I returned to my apartment and then we walked and looked at the city, something I rarely if ever do.

In Central Park, we toured the lake, zoo, great lawn and emerged on Fifth Avenue. We walked along Fifth from 81st Street to 42nd Street, stopping at Rockefeller Center, Saint Patrick's Cathedral and had a late lunch in a coffee shop inside Grand Central Station.

We hit the West Side and Times Square and checked out the Disney Store and some others.

"How would you like a fifteen dollar cup of coffee?" I asked as we walked past the Marriot Hotel.

"That's a bit extravagant isn't it?" Ellen said.

"It comes with a view," I said.

I took her to the View Lounge in the Marriott Marquis in Times Square, located on the rooftop. The entire lounge revolves so the view changes every few seconds. We grabbed a table for two beside a window and drank two cups of coffee as the city rotated around us.

"I've missed a lot," Ellen said as we returned to Broadway.

"We all have," I said.

"I'll need to go home," she said.

It was just a short walk back to the apartment.

Ellen gathered up her things in the bedroom. When her bag was packed she looked up at me. I could see the anger boiling in her eyes.

"Goddamn you, Kellerman," she said.

A storm was brewing. I waited for it to hit.

Ellen yanked open my pants and removed them, then placed her hands on my chest and shoved me onto the bed. The cats, sleeping, awoke and ran for cover.

Ellen pulled off her blouse and pants and sat on my legs. Her eyes glared angrily at me. She wiggled her way onto my stomach, then chest until she was directly over my face.

Then she lowered herself and I let her.

*****

"I'm not sorry I did that," Ellen said as I drove us across the Verazzano.

"Me neither," I said. "I am curious as to why you're so mad though."

"Because I'm falling in love and I don't want to," she said. "I don't want to but it's happening anyway."

"I already told you things between us can be good," I said.

"Good isn't love," Ellen said. "Can you love a woman as screwed up as I am?"

"I think so, yes."

"Prove it," Ellen said. "Go with me to a meeting and then kiss me good night like a gentleman at the door."

We made an eight o'clock meeting at the church near her house and then I drove Ellen home and kissed her at the door.

"I'll call you tomorrow night after I meet with Ira," I said.

"Thank you," Ellen said. "For everything."

*****

"I heard a rumor you fell in love and left town," Johnny said as he served up a mug of coffee.

"I've been working," I said.

"Yeah, yeah, and I saw the work coming and going a few times," Johnny said.

"Ira will be by seven-thirty tomorrow night," I said. "I'd like Hawkins to be present as well."

"Larkin?"

"Not yet," I said. "I'll fill him in afterwards."

"That fifty thousand is burning a hole in my safe," Johnny said.

"Let it sit for a while," I said.

"Feel like losing a game?" Johnny said.

Fifty-one moves later, after I toppled my king, I licked my wounds and crawled into bed and with the cats for company, drifted off to sleep.

Chapter Twenty-six

After a light breakfast, I pounded out a ninety minute workout at the Y, then borrowed Mrs. Parker's phone to call Hawkins.

"I found some documents of interest in Fallen's old files," I said. "I doubt they add up to much, but I'll let you decide that."

"Bring them by, I'll take a look," Hawkins said.

"I'll give them to you tonight at seven-thirty at the Pub when we meet with Ira the computer hacker," I said. "Otherwise known as Warlord Emperor."

"Warlord Emperor?"

"Catchy, isn't it?"

Hawkins sighed.

"Don't be late," I said.

I returned the phone to Mrs. Parker.

"We had a wonderful brunch," she said. "My grandchildren are all teenagers now. We went to the Carnegie Deli. It's a bit pricy, but the food is wonderful."

"I'm glad you enjoyed yourself," I said.

When I returned to my apartment the cats were moping around at the window.

"She's not here, boys," I said.

I perked them up with some catnip, then changed into another set of sweats. Before I left the apartment, I ate a peanut butter sandwich with a glass of orange juice.

Roth's Gym was crowded with the usual array of wannabe fighters making a nuisance of themselves.

I grabbed a rope and jumped for thirty minutes while I waited for the amateurs to clear out. When a speed bag was free I went to work on that for thirty minutes, then switched out to the hundred pound heavy bag and worked that for another thirty.

When I was done, I found Roth seated ringside watching a pair of middleweights slog around the ring.

"How did your welterweight fare in his six rounder?" I asked.

"Got off the canvas in the first, third and fifth rounds to win by a knockout in the sixth," Roth said.

"Sounds like your boy has heart," I said.

"To go with his glass chin," Roth said.

"As they say in sports, a win is a win," I said.

*****

I took a forty-five minute nap followed by a hot shower. I dressed in jeans and tee-shirt and a summer windbreaker and went down to the bar at seven twenty-five. Johnny was at a booth with Hawkins. Both were drinking bourbon.

"Shall we wait for our friend in the office?" Johnny said.

Ira was ten minutes late. When he was shown into the office by Cindy, he said, "Subway was backed up. Delayed for twenty minutes."

"No problem," I said from behind the desk. "So what do you got?"

Johnny stood beside his file cabinet, dug out his bottle and an extra glass and poured Ira a drink.

Ira nodded and then looked at Hawkins who was seated in one of two chairs. "Who's this?" Ira asked.

"Hawkins. The attorney I work for," I said.

Ira nodded again and took the vacant chair.

I lit a cigarette.

"They have a very secure network," Ira said. "I had less trouble hacking the Social Security Department."

"You hacked the ... why?" Hawkins said.

"My mom retired at sixty-two and gets the minimum," Ira said. "I pushed a few buttons and gave her a raise. She don't know that of course."

"Secret's safe with me," Hawkins said.

I blew a smoke ring and waited.

"Of course it's safe with you, you don't know my mom," Ira said.

"I meant … it's a figure of … never mind," Hawkins said.

"Nobody fucks with a guy's mom," Ira said.

"Ira, Warlord Emperor, what have you got for me?" I said.

Ira reached into the inside pocket of the windbreaker he was wearing and produced an envelope and set it on the desk.

"Once I got in it was a hot knife through butter," Ira said. "I checked back two years and cross referenced everything against the list of names you gave me plus their own internal records and Bingo, the end result is in that envelope."

I reached for the envelope and removed two folded sheets of paper. The first paper showed twenty-three wire transfers made by a Michael Ross Jr. in the amount of one thousand per transfer.

Each transfer was made during the first week of each month and scattered through out the East Coast clear to Kansas City. The sender used several Western Union outlets in Queens and a few in Manhattan.

The recipient of each transfer had a different name, but two of the names came off Ellen's list.

That's how Ira located Michael Ross Jr.

I flipped to the second page. It had Ross's bio.

I set the papers down and pulled out the envelope from my windbreaker and set it on the desk.

"Thirteen thousand," I said. "Consider the extra five hundred a contribution to your mother's social security."

"Thanks," Ira said.

After Ira left, I showed the two documents to Hawkins.

Johnny had a small copy machine in the corner of the office and I made copies for Hawkins.

I gave them the copies along with the documents from Fallen's files at Ellen's house. "I'll call you tomorrow after I speak with Larkin," I said.

After Hawkins left, I played a quick game with Johnny at a booth. The kitchen had meatloaf and we each had double portions while we played.

"You played well tonight," Johnny said when he placed me in checkmate after sixty-seven moves.

I took the compliment to his office and called Ellen.

"I was getting worried you wouldn't call," she said.

"We have a solid lead," I said. "Ira …"

"The Warlord Emperor guy?"

"Yeah, him. He found two names Cosby used in the past receiving payments of one thousand a month from someone named Michael Ross Jr.," I said. "Twenty-three payments so far using wire transfers."

"So Brian is still alive?"

"Appears so and maybe this Ross can steer us to your son."

"Could that be possible?"

"Anything is possible," I said.

"I'm having a moment of weakness here," Ellen said. "Tell me to be strong."

"You have to be strong or I can't do this," I said.

"I want to get high in the worst way," Ellen said.

"Don't."

"I won't. There's a ten pm meeting at the church," Ellen said. "Can we get together on Wednesday?"

"We can. Where?"

"My place. We can finish my father's files. I get home right around six."

"I'll be there."

"And I'll make dinner," Ellen said.

When I left Johnny's office, I went back to the apartment and sat at the table and read Ira's reports a second time.

Michael Ross Jr's age was listed at thirty-seven. His profession was certified public accountant. He had an office on Queens Boulevard in the wealthy neighborhood of Forest Hills. He was married with two children, a boy age eleven and a nine-year-old girl. His wife was a history teacher at Forest Hills High School.

She made close to eighty thousand a year teaching.

Michael pulled in an average of a hundred and twenty-five thousand a year from his accounting business.

Not millionaires, but well off and comfortable.

Would Michael miss a grand a month?

Probably not.

My initial thought was why Michael Ross Jr. would pay a thousand a month to junkie Brian Cosby?

The connection came in the form of Michael Ross Senior, age listed as sixty-seven and a practicing private adoption attorney for thirty years. Originally from Staten Island, Ross Senior had offices on Staten Island and in Forest Hills in Queens.

According to Ira's report, Ross Senior stopped paying taxes five years ago and started drawing social security.

Ross Senior's last known address was a home in Forest Hills, the same address as his son's.

Senior retired and moved in with his son.

Ross paid the ransom every month for peace of mind in his old age and for no other reason.

I set the papers aside and smoked a cigarette at the window.

When I went to bed, the cats were already entwined into a ball near Ellen's pillow.

I put me head down and the cats looked at me.

"Yeah, I can smell her too," I told them.

Chapter Twenty-seven

On my way to breakfast, I called Larkin on his cell phone.

"Free for lunch?" I asked. "I have something quite interesting to run by you."

"Do you like ribs?"

"Who doesn't?"

"Meet me at Mama's in Harlem at one o'clock," Larkin said.

From breakfast, I walked to the Y and got in a ninety minute workout in the gym. An hour in the weight room and thirty minutes on the track.

I jogged home and played with the cats for a bit after giving them a dose of catnip.

When the crashed and burned, I shaved and took a shower. I selected a light grey summer suit and wore it with a white tee-shirt.

There was no way I was fighting with noon traffic going uptown, so I grabbed a cab and let the driver do the fighting for me.

The ride to One Hundred and Twenty-Fifth Street took twenty-five minutes. The distance was just three miles.

The Adam Clayton Powell Jr. building dominates the neighborhood. A nineteen story structure that was home to many government departments. A few years back, former president Bill Clinton had an office in Harlem, but I heard he move it downtown.

One Twenty-Fifth was lined with street merchants selling everything from portraits to rugs.

The line to get into Mama's was out the door and mostly white. I entered and went to the reservations podium where an attractive black woman was on duty.

"I'm meeting Police Captain Larkin at one, is he here yet?" I asked her.

"He's already here," she said. "The table against the wall on the street side."

"Thank you."

Larkin was nibbling on bread and sipping scotch over ice when I joined him at the table for six that he occupied alone.

"Ever had the ribs in this place? Best in the City," he said.

"I haven't," I said.

There were about sixty tables with seventy percent white patrons.

"So, what's your news?" Larkin said. "I haven't had much luck poking around on my own, so I could use some good news."

I withdrew Ira's documents from my pocket and set them on the table. "A direct link to Brian Cosby, the man he's blackmailing and both tie into an illegal baby selling operation," I said.

A waitress came by and we ordered the ribs special, a Coke for me and another scotch for Larkin.

He read the documents while we waited for the food.

"I won't ask how you came by this information," Larkin said when he read through both pages.

"This is a two-for," I said. "You get to haul in a wanted murderer and kidnapper and arrest the attorney who is involved in selling babies."

Larkin looked at me. "We discussed it, but what do you get?"

"I'm being paid by my client," I said. "Her son gets his inheritance and I don't expect to even get mentioned. In fact, I'd prefer not to."

"I'll need a cover story," Larkin said.

"Attorney Cal Hawkins, an old family friend of the Fallen's was asked for help by Ellen Fallen in getting her son's inheritance to her son and Hawkins, an old friend of yours came to you for help," I said. "You took it upon yourself to reopen an old case and what do you know, you were successful."

Larkin sipped his scotch, looked at me and then said, "That could actually pass the smell test."

"We need to get to Ross Jr.," I said. "And before he makes the next wire transfer."

"Did you bring your car?"

"Cab."

"We'll take mine," Larkin said.

The waitress brought us our ribs, huge racks of fall off the bone tender.

We took our time eating and every bite was pure joy for a ribs lover.

When the check came, Larkin didn't move and I paid the bill with a hundred plus a twenty dollar tip.

*****

"Go ahead and smoke," Larkin said. "It won't bother me none."

I lowered my window first and then lit up. Larkin took the bridge into Queens and found Queens Boulevard and headed us north. When we reached Forest Hills, we poked around a bit until we located the six-story office building where Ross Jr. had his office.

We parked in the small lot that faced the railroad stop on the Amtrak Line.

"It's four o'clock, we should hang back a bit and try to catch him alone in his office," Larkin said. "We'll give him until four-thirty."

There was a little coffee shop across the street and I grabbed two containers and we drank them in Larkin's car.

At four-thirty, we entered the building. Ross Jr. had his office on the sixth floor. Larkin led the way and didn't knock when he opened the door and entered the office.

The reception desk was empty. A short hallway led to another door and Larkin opened it and we found Michael Ross Jr. behind a desk piled high with paperwork.

Ross Jr. looked up at us. He was a slim man with a slightly receding hairline with reading glasses perched on his nose. He removed the glasses and said, "May I help you?"

Larkin showed his badge. "Captain Larkin. This is my associate Kellerman. We have a few questions to ask you Mr. Ross."

"Questions?" Ross said. "What about?"

"About the money you pay each month to a known kidnapper and murderer in the form of blackmail," Larkin said.

"I … I don't know what you're talking about," Ross Jr. said.

"No?" Larkin said. "Brian Cosby was stupid enough to use some fake names that he used in the past to pick up the money you wire him every month. That's how we traced it back to you."

"I want to call my lawyer," Ross Jr. said.

"If you do that I'll have to arrest you," Larkin said. "Do you really want all your business associates in the building to see you led out of here in handcuffs?"

Ross Jr. sighed.

"We know you're covering for your father," I said. "Talk to us here or downtown, which?"

Ross Jr. sighed again.

"Third option," I said. "I open the window there beside your desk and dangle you from your ankles until you decide to talk to us."

"You can't do that," Ross Jr. said.

"I'm not a cop," I said. "I can do whatever the fuck I want."

I walked to the window. It was the type that didn't open. I grabbed the phone off the desk.

"Guess I just have to break it," I said.

"Stop," Ross Jr. said. "Just stop."

"Talk to us," I said and replaced the phone.

"I didn't know about my father's transgressions until two years ago when this Brian Cosby showed up at the house," Ross Jr. said. "It used to be my dad's house before he was hit with advanced dementia. He now is in the beginning stages of Alzheimer's. I had to move him to an assisted living facility for Alzheimer and dementia patients."

"What did Cosby tell you?" I asked.

"That he made some kind of deal with my father to bring him a baby to sell on the black market," Ross Jr. said. "He said my father had done it before, many times. He said if I didn't pay him he would leak the story to the police. My father would spend his last years in prison, my name would be ruined, and my family would suffer. I decided to pay."

"How do you know when and where to wire the money?" I asked.

"He calls. Right here. Usually at the end of the month with a location and name," Ross said.

I looked at Larkin. He nodded.

"We don't want you," I said. "We want Brian Cosby and we want to speak with your father about the baby Cosby kidnapped. We'll keep your name out of it as much as possible."

"Do you have a car?" Ross Jr. asked.

"We do. We'll take yours," I said.

Ross Jr. nodded and picked up the phone. He dialed a number and said, "Hi, honey. I'll be a bit late tonight. I decided to pop over and see dad for a bit. Talk to you later. Love you."

He hung up the phone.

"Let's go," Ross Jr. said.

*****

The facility was located in Hillcrest Estates, an area where the United Nations once had housing for diplomats. It was a nice enough place with gardens, lawns and trees.

It doesn't matter how nice a place like this is though, when you walk through the doors it smells like death.

After checking us in, Ross Jr. led us through a maze of hallways to his father's room.

It was empty.

Ross Jr. used the intercom on the wall to call a nurse. One arrived almost immediately.

"Where is my father?" Ross Jr. demanded.

"Oh, relax sir, he's in the garden with others enjoying the fresh air," the nurse said. "The door to the garden is …"

"I know where it is, thanks," Ross Jr. said.

He led us down another maze of hallways to glass doors that opened to an acre or more garden.

About fifty residents were in the garden, seated on benches, in chairs or standing. Several nurses stood watch.

"There he is on that bench," Ross Jr. said.

Ross Sr. was at complete peace. It showed in his brown eyes that no one was home. He had snowy white hair and hadn't been shaved in several days. He seemed to be watching some birds at a feeder.

"Dad, it's Mike," Ross Jr. said.

"I've noticed that the birds appear to take turns at the feeder," Ross Sr. said. "One waits until the one at the feeder is done and then they switch places. I've noticed that before."

"Dad, it's Mike," Ross Jr. said. "Your son."

Ross Sr. looked at me. "My son?"

"No, Dad, me," Ross Jr. said. "I'm Michael, your son."

Ross Sr. looked at the bird feeder. "See how the big red bird chases away the tiny yellow one."

Ross Jr. looked at me. "See how it is?"

I nodded.

"Dad, how are you feeling?" Ross Jr. asked.

"The tiny yellow one patiently waits his turn," Ross Sr. said. "There is an order to it, but I can't figure out what it is exactly."

"That's okay, Dad," Ross Jr. said.

I looked at Larkin.

"We're done here," I said.

*****

"There are two days left in the month," I said as Ross. Jr. drove us back to his office. "By what you said he'll call tomorrow or the next day."

"And always right around noon," Ross Jr. said.

"I'll sit with you and when he calls you put it on speaker phone," I said. I turned and looked at Larkin in the back seat. "Know anybody at the FBI who won't mind an easy pickup?"

"I know a few at the district office downtown," Larkin said.

"As soon as I have Cosby's location for the wire transfer, I'll call you and they can pick him up," I said. "They can ship him back, federally charge him with kidnapping and you slap the murder charge on him."

"That's all good, but how does it help your client find the kidnapped boy?" Larkin asked.

"It doesn't," I said. I looked at Ross Jr. "When he retired, his files went where?"

"Everywhere," Ross Jr. said. "Divided among six or seven adoption attorney's throughout the city. I would tend to think if there were any improprieties I would have been made aware of them by now."

"Two sets of books?" I said.

"If there are, I never saw them," Ross Jr. said.

"What about personal belongings from his office that he kept?"

"A couple of boxes in the garage," Ross Jr. said. "I've never even gone through them."

"Bring them to the office tomorrow," I said. "We'll go through them tomorrow while we wait for Cosby's call."

At Larkin's car, Larkin said, "If there is a leak, I will have you picked up for aiding and abetting a known fugitive."

"So you believe I want my life ruined, my business ruined, my wife disgraced and my children ridiculed at school, is that what you think?" Ross Jr. said.

"Just play this straight and nobody gets hurt but the bad guys," Larkin said.

"My father is one of the bad guys," Ross Jr. said.

"Nobody in their right mind would drag him into court," Larkin said.

"What time do you usually show up for work?" I asked Ross Jr.

"Around nine-thirty," Ross Jr. said. "My receptionist is on maternal leave, so I'll be alone."

"I'll see you at nine-thirty," I said.

*****

On the drive back to Manhattan, Larkin said, "I'll make some calls when I get back to the office. Then I'll wait by the phone for your call."

"If I don't call you by five, it's a no show and we'll do it again on Thursday," I said.

Larkin nodded.

"Drop me off at the Pub," I said.

*****

I called Helen from Johnny's office.

"I just walked in the door not five minutes ago," she said.

"There's been a breakthrough," I said.

I took five minutes to give Ellen the short version.

"Do you really think it's possible to catch this heartless bastard after all these years?" Ellen asked when I concluded.

"Not possible," I said. "Likely."

"I'd love a ringside seat at his trial," Ellen said.

"You'll do better than that if you testify," I said. "But that's down the road. I could be stuck tomorrow and not make it until Thursday."

"I understand," Ellen said. "I'm not happy about it, but I understand."

"I'll call you as soon as I know one way or the other," I said.

Ellen sighed. "It's not the one way that bothers me, it's the other," she said.

After I got off the phone with Ellen, I had a cup of coffee at the bar with Johnny.

"I'll take that check now," I said.

"Out of expense money?" Johnny asked.

"I'll take what I need from the check," I said.

"It will be our secret," Johnny said.

"How about a game and some food?" I said.

Several hours later when I licked my wounds after having lost the match to Johnny in forty-nine moves, I found another from Davis in my mailbox.

I opened it on the sofa.

King's knight to Bishop one. And send mo books.

Well, at least it wasn't a death threat.

Chapter Twenty-eight

"It seems to be all junk," Ross Jr. said.

We were eating fried egg sandwiches with hash browns and coffee.

"Not to him or he wouldn't have kept it," I said. "What about his will, bank accountants and tax returns."

"The other box there on the floor."

I switched out the boxes. This one was loaded with the good stuff. The house in Forest Hills had been signed over to Jr. in the form of a living will and was valued at just over one million dollars and carried no mortgage.

"It's Forest Hills," Ross Jr. said of the excessive price tag on the house.

There was a life insurance policy for five hundred thousand with Ross Jr. as the beneficiary. A savings account had one hundred thousand in it and a Roth IRA had another one hundred thousand, both with Ross Jr. as the beneficiary. There was a stock portfolio worth about fifty grand.

Tax returns for the last seven years Ross Sr. was in business showed he averaged about two hundred and fifty thousand a year in income.

"Your father did very well," I said.

"He did."

"How much does that home he's in cost a month?"

"Nine thousand," Ross Jr. said. "They take his social security check and I make up the difference. There was another insurance police for two hundred and fifty thousand that I turned over to them and when that's gone, I start using his savings, IRA and so on."

I sipped some coffee and thought for a few minutes while Ross Jr. continued shuffling papers.

"Do you know what I don't see?" I said. "Where he stashed his illegal money."

Ross Jr. nodded. "It would need to be accounted for if he channeled it into his legal funds or the IRS would have audited him."

I picked up a thick manila envelope from the bottom of the box. "What's this?"

"Dad packed this box before he was too far gone," Ross Jr. said. "He was still living in the house at the time."

I opened the envelope and dumped the contents. One gold watch, Rolex. One gold bracelet. One wedding ring. One Italian wallet, imported.

We went through the wallet. Six credit cards all expired. Some family photographs. Driver's license also expired. Social Security card. One thousand dollars in fifties and twenties.

One set of keys.

I picked up the key ring and did an inventory. One car key.

"The car?" I said.

"Sold it a few years ago," Ross Jr. said. "A nice BMW. I put the money towards dad's care at the home."

"This key?"

"The house. I should probably take that one."

"This?"

"Looks like his old office key. He had both offices keyed alike."

The remaining key I recognized immediately.

"This?"

Ross Jr. shook his head. "Don't know."

"It's for a safe deposit box," I said. I turned the key over. "Bank of Manhattan. Box 118."

I picked up the wallet again and took everything out. There was a secret flap where the cash was stored. I lifted the flap and removed the small card that identified the key holder as the bearer of the box.

"Meet me at the bank tomorrow morning at nine," I said and tucked the key and card into my pocket.

"What do you suppose is in there?" Ross Jr. asked.

"Whatever it is belongs to you," I said.

"I'm not sure I want to know," Ross Jr. said.

"Do you know what I think Mr. Ross?" I said. "I think your father knew he was losing it and destroyed any records he had of his illegal transactions."

"I fear you might be correct," Ross Jr. said.

I glanced at my watch. "An hour before noon. Want another coffee?"

"Why not?"

I went downstairs and cross the street to the little coffee shop. I smoked a cigarette, then went in for two containers and returned to Ross Jr.

"Thanks," he said when I gave him a container. "I was thinking while you were gone. Do you think my father may have kept a list of his illegal ... I'm not sure what to call them."

"Call them transactions for now."

"Right. Do you suppose he kept a list and it's in the safe deposit box?"

"I wouldn't, but you never know what somebody might do," I said. "We'll find out tomorrow."

We drank our coffee in silence as we waited for the phone to ring.

Ten minutes before noon, Ross Jr. began to sweat. He wiped his face and hands on a napkin.

"I'm always as nervous on a cat on a hot tin roof before he calls," he said. "Even though it's been two years, I still get a sick feeling in my gut."

"You have a great deal to lose," I said. "Tell me something, since you had no idea what you father was up to and there are no records of it, when he contacted you, why did you believe him?"

"He called the house looking for dad," Ross Jr. said. "At first he identified himself as a former client. When I told him dad had been hospitalized, he went into great detail concerning dad's activities in the black market. He told me about this one incident where a baby was kidnapped, the grandmother murdered and my father sold the baby to a couple for one hundred and fifty thousand. He described my father and his Staten Island office in detail, right down to the photos on his desk. He told me to check out the story and he'd call back the next day. I checked and the story was accurate. The next day, instead of calling, he showed up on my doorstep. He said that was to let me know he knew where I lived and what I looked like and that he could get to my family if I didn't cooperate."

"What did he look like?" I asked.

"Tall, thin, full beard and long hair. He wore one of those green Army jackets. He had a gun. I saw the butt sticking up from his pants."

"Seen him since?"

No. It's always by phone. What would you have done?"

"I would have thrown him off a roof and let him rot," I said.

Ross Jr. looked at me. "I guess you would," he said.

The phone rang and Ross Jr. scooped it up. "Michael Ross," he said.

He hit the speaker phone button and Cosby said, "It's me, Mr. Ross. Wire station at the Walgreens number 999955. I'll pick it up on Friday at noon."

Cosby hung up and we listened to the hum for a few seconds until Ross Jr. set the phone down.

"Where is that?" I said. "Can you find out?"

Ross Jr. turned to his computer and checked Western Union locations.

"West Warwick, Rhode Island," he said.

I picked up the phone and called Larkin. "A Walgreens in Warwick, Rhode Island," I said. "Noon on Friday." I looked at the computer and read the address.

"I've already called some friends at the FBI," Larkin said. "They said they'd be glad to pick him up and work the kidnapping angle. I get the murder beef. Marshals will transport him to New York; he should be here by Saturday."

"I want in on the interrogation," I said.

"I'll get Deputy Inspector out of this, you've earned that."

"I'll call you Friday," I said. "You can give me details then."

After I hung up, I thought for a moment and said, "Do you have any pressing business this afternoon?"

"Quarterly tax reports for several clients," Ross Jr. said. "Nothing that can't wait."

"Let's go," I said.

"Where?"

"Banking."

*****

"I'm sweating like a pig," Ross Jr. said.

I took Queens Boulevard south across the 59th Street Bridge into Manhattan.

"Pigs don't sweat," I said. "That's why they roll around in mud, to cool off their skin."

"I feel sick," Ross Jr. said.

"We're going to a bank, not the death penalty chamber," I said.

"I'm afraid of what I might find," Ross Jr. said.

"Just relax," I said. "The bank is on Forty-ninth and Sixth. We can grab some air across the street at the little park at an office building."

I put the car in a lot on Sixth and we walked the one block to the office building across the street from the bank.

We found an empty bench and sat. I fired up a cigarette.

It was just a few minutes past two in the afternoon.

"The vault for safe deposit boxes is in the basement," I said. "We go in, I show the card and key and we get brought down to the vault room where an attendant brings us box 118. Whatever is in it no one but us will know."

"What if it's evidence against my father?"

"If it doesn't help my client, destroy it," I said. "You heard what Larkin said about prosecuting your father."

Ross Jr. nodded. He took a deep breath and said, "I'm ready."

*****

The vault attendant carried box 118 to a private viewing station, set it on the table and told us to call him when we were ready.

I opened the lid and looked at the twelve stacks of one hundred dollar bills that were inside the box.

There was nothing else except the money.

I picked up one stack. It was fifty thousand dollars by the thickness of it.

"How much is in there?" Ross Jr. asked.

"Six hundred thousand," I said.

"What do we do with it?"

"We don't do anything with it," I said. "It belongs to you, do with it what you wish."

"It's dirty money," Ross Jr. said. "It should be returned."

"And who would you return it to? You could donate it to charity, but how would you explain it to the IRS. You could turn it over to the police and guess how fast it would disappear? You could give it to the government and it would wind up in some corrupt official's pocket. Keep the money for a rainy day, Mr. Ross. You have my word no one else will know."

"I can't imagine the evil my father did to compile this kind of money," Ross Jr. said.

"Don't think about it," I said. "Put your kids through college; secure your old age, whatever. Just don't flash it up and spend all over town. The IRS isn't stupid."

Ross Jr. nodded. "I'll leave it here for now."

*****

In front of the bank, I shook hands with Ross Jr.

"Have money for a cab?" I asked.

"I do."

"See you on Friday," I said.

Ross Jr. nodded. "Thanks," he said. "For everything."

I retrieved my car, drove home and quickly changed into workout gear. I left the apartment and jogged over to the Y and put myself through a brutal ninety minute workout.

I quit when I couldn't do one more rep in the weight room and lap on the track and then headed back to the apartment.

After a shower and change of clothes, I returned to my car and headed for Staten Island.

*****

Ellen answered her door wearing a grey tee-shirt that came down to her knees and white socks. Her hair was still damp from a recent shower. The smile on her lips was one of relief and gladness.

"I was worried," she said as she did her best to hug and kiss me.

I scooped her up in my arms and carried her to the sofa and sat her down.

She looked at me as I got down on my knees.

"I'm on fire," I said.

"Me too," Ellen whispered.

She lifted the tee-shirt and parted her legs to show me she wasn't wearing panties. I leaned in close. She was sopping wet. I took a small taste and Ellen put her hands on my hair and leaned back and closed her eyes.

"Do it," she said.

*****

"I can hardly walk," Ellen said as we took mugs of coffee to the backyard patio table.

We sat and I lit a cigarette.

"You have to understand that on a full stomach I'm a hundred and eleven pounds at best," Ellen said. "You can't split me like Abe Lincoln splitting rails and expect me to walk around normally afterward."

"Was I that rough?"

"Your strength is incredible," Ellen said.

"Next time you lead," I said.

"Just take it easy on the me Tarzan you Jane, okay?"

I inhaled smoke, blew a ring and said, "Are you ready for some news?"

Ellen looked at me. "Good or bad?"

I told her about the phone call, the Friday wire transfer and the FBI involvement to pick up Brian Cosby.

"After all these years I will finally get to spit in his face," Ellen said. "Do you think he'll know who my baby was sold to?"

"If he's smart he'll use the information to plea bargain," I said.

"I never thought we'd get this far," Ellen said. "What you said in the beginning, you deserve far more than what I gave you."

"I'm not in this for a payday," I said. "This is for you."

"But we had an …"

"Had," I said. "Us becoming an us changes things."

Ellen stared at me for a moment. "That fifty thousand, you're using it for expenses, aren't you?"

"Does it matter? "I said. "The goal is to get the inheritance to your son. We becoming an us is a bonus."

Ellen nodded.

"I'm hungry," she said.

*****

Six candles flickered light as I stripped down in the bathroom. Ellen, already in the tub looked at me.

"How many times have you been shot?" she said as she looked at my scars.

I stepped over the rim into the how water and slowly sat down. "Four," I said.

Ellen touched the two scars just above my right pec, the one on my left side and then said, "Where's the fourth?"

"Lower back on the left side."

She traced a thin line on my right rib cage. "This?"

"Cut from a straight razor."

Ellen shook her head. "Legs?"

"Small wounds from grenade shrapnel."

"My scars are pinpricks, mostly and too faded to really notice," Ellen said. "I do have a rather prominent birthmark though."

"Where?"

"You tell me, your nose was buried in it a little while ago."

Except for her neck and head, Ellen was below the water line.

"X marks the spot," she said.

*****

Naked, Ellen sat on her bed and smirked at me as I searched for her birthmark.

"Open," I said.

Ellen parted her legs. The birthmark was a tiny, near perfect bluish leaf on her left inside thigh.

"X doesn't mark the spot," I said. "But the V does."

Chapter Twenty-nine

After Ellen went to work, I drove home and changed into comfortable sweats. I fed and watered the cats and then gave them some catnip before I ventured out to Roth's gym.

I divided a ninety minute workout between jump rope, speed bag and heavy bag. Afterward, I sat with Roth and watched a pair of sluggish heavyweight's pitty-pat each other for three rounds.

"Jesus God if you goons don't start fighting I'm going to have Kellerman come up their and wipe the floor with the both of you bums," Roth shouted.

"Hey, fuck you pop," one of them snapped at Roth.

Roth looked at me.

I jumped up from my chair, stepped onto the milk crate that served as a step and climbed into the ring.

"You, out," I said to the other heavyweight. "You, bigmouth, Roth was fighting fifteen rounders before you were dribble leaking out of your mother's hole."

The other heavyweight got the hell out of the ring. The gym went quiet as every fighter working out stopped to watch.

The bigmouth looked at me. He had on full sparring gear. "You wanna go, you need gear. That's the rule."

"I don't need gear for a pussy like you," I said.

He looked at me. I could see the scared in his eyes, but his mouth got him into a situation his pride couldn't get out of.

"Suit yourself," he said.

I didn't bother with jabs or defense. As soon as he moved, I hit him with a left hook, a straight right, another hook and as he went down to one knee, I backhanded him across the mouth.

He spilled onto his stomach and I kicked him in the ribs.

"If I ever catch you in here again I guarantee you'll spend the rest of your life in a wheelchair," I said and for good measure, I kicked him again.

I stepped out of the ring and walked to the locker room.

"What are you mugs looking at, get back to work," Roth yelled.

*****

After lunch, I drove a carton of new books to give Davis at the prison.

He looked better.

"You've been working out," I said.

"It hard to get a real workout at this dump," Davis said. "Shitty equipment plus bad food and no supplements. You bring my books?"

"Gave them to the guard," I said. "And a note with my next move."

"You know, I ain't gonna feel good about killing you when I get outta here," Davis said.

"Don't forget our agreement," I said. "You can't kill me until I get you back in shape."

"Yeah, yeah, I remember," Davis said. "How things with your lady?"

"She's gone. Put her house up for sale."

"Sorry to hear that."

"I have a new lady though," I said. "I wasn't expecting it, it just sort of happened."

"That the best way."

"You'll like her. She has the guts of a burglar."

Davis nodded. "Thanks for the books, man. I mail you my next move."

I hung up the phone and watched the guard take Davis out of the visitor's center.

*****

"I was just on my way out," Hawkins said.

"Buy you a drink?" I said.

"You have news?"

"I do."

"There's a bar around the corner that serves a decent cup of coffee," Hawkins said.

*****

"Son of a bitch, Kellerman," Hawkins said.

"It will take some plotting, but I think all involved will go for it. Ellen is a material witness and you are her attorney."

"Why not let me call Larkin and the FBI?" Hawkins suggested.

"I didn't say otherwise," I said. "Just make sure you do it first thing tomorrow morning. Larkin will be with me at noon, so get him around nine."

Hawkins nodded. "I feel the need to ask you a personal question," he said.

I sipped some coffee and said, "Ask."

"Has something developed between you and Ellen?"

"That has no bearing on this," I said.

"For God's sake, don't hurt her," Hawkins said. "She's been through more than enough for one lifetime."

"Ellen is tougher that you, me and Davis put together," I said.

Hawking nodded. "Alright," he said. "We'll speak again tomorrow."

*****

"I'll need you to drive to my place tomorrow after work," I said. "Plan on at least until Monday."

I could hear Ellen breathing hard over Mrs. Parker's phone. "What's going to happen?" she finally asked.

"Hopefully a lot," I said.

"Okay," she said as she sighed.

"Not to worry," I said. "I'll be by your side the entire time and he won't even see you."

"I can be there by six-thirty," Ellen said.

"Okay. If something happens, call the Pub and speak to Johnny," I said. "Otherwise, I'll see you at six-thirty."

I returned the phone to Mrs. Parker and entered my apartment and changed into clean sweats.

The Y stayed open late and I was able to get in a full ninety minute workout. On the way home, I stopped at the Cuban restaurant and grabbed a steak to go.

I ate while reading the newspaper sports section.

Afterward, I smoked a few cigarettes at the bedroom window and watched the street. A slight mist had developed and the colors of the night reflected on the street and sidewalk.

The City needed a good rain to wash away the stink.

You could say that about a lot of things in life.

Chapter Thirty

I dressed casually and took the Lincoln to Queens and arrived at Ross Jr's office by nine in the morning.

He car wasn't in his spot.

I got out of the Lincoln and smoked a cigarette in the shade of the building.

Ross Jr. arrived at nine-fifteen.

"I needed to withdraw funds from the bank," he said. "That's why I'm a bit late."

"Had breakfast?"

He shook his head.

"Go on up. I'll get some."

I crossed the street to the little coffee shop and ordered egg and bacon sandwiches with hash browns and coffee.

Ross Jr. was in his office. He had removed his jacket and rolled up his sleeves and was looking out the window.

"How come you didn't hire a temporary receptionist?" I asked.

"If this were January, I'd get a temp, but I can get by on my own for a few weeks." Ross Jr. said.

We ate at his desk.

"I've been thinking about the money in the safe deposit box," Ross Jr. said. "It's impossible to hide even one penny of declared income from the IRS. That's something I know about. If I gave it to charity in large amounts I would have to somehow have to account for it in my income. If I invested it, same thing. My father must have known this or he wouldn't have hid it in the bank."

"That's always the problem with ill-gotten gains, hiding it from the IRS," I said. "You and your wife have a good income so if you took thirty thousand of it a year and invested twenty of it into college funds and ten into your retirement account, the IRS shouldn't blink at that."

"Are you speaking from experience?" Ross Jr. asked.

"Let's just say I live under the radar and leave it at that," I said.

After we ate, Ross Jr. busied himself with some work while I went downstairs for a cigarette.

Larkin arrived close to eleven and he parked next to my Lincoln.

"A lot of phone calls and arrangements to be made this morning," he said. "That Hawkins could talk the scales off a snake."

"And the bottom like is?"

"I do the interrogation along with an FBI agent," Larkin said. "You, Hawkins and the girl get to watch."

"Good."

"Ross?"

"In his office sweating it out."

"Let me go say hi," Larkin said.

*****

We walked to the drug store on Queens Boulevard where Ross Jr. wired the money to Cosby.

We were back in Ross Jr's office by twelve twenty.

Larkin's cell phone rang ten minutes later.

He identified himself, listened, said thank you and hung up.

"FBI picked him up," Larkin said. "He'll be flown to New York late this afternoon. Interrogation begins at noon on Saturday. Son of a Bitch."

"Congratulations Deputy Inspector," I said.

"Not yet, but I'm closer," Larkin said. "Mr. Ross, are you prepared to be a material witness?"

Ross Jr. nodded.

"I'll be in touch," Larkin said.

"Hang in there Mr. Ross," I said.

*****

I smoked a cigarette and chatted with Larkin in the parking lot.

"He's not a bad fellow," Larkin said. "He needn't feel ashamed because of his father."

"He knows that," I said.

Larkin looked at me.

"You would have made a helluva cop," he said.

"God forbid," I said.

*****

I took a ninety minute workout at the Y and was back in my apartment by four-thirty. I showered and put on some casual clothes and went down to the Pub to wait for Ellen.

At a booth, I gave Johnny an update.

He was drinking his usual bourbon to my coffee.

"I have to admit I didn't think you would pull this one off," he said.

"I haven't yet," I said. "The job was to deliver the inheritance to Ellen's son. All I've done so far in reel in a junkie."

"That's more than the FBI and police could do," Johnny said.

I glanced at my watch. "More to follow," I said.

I went to the parking lot to wait for Ellen. Traffic was clogged with Friday night commuters and she was late. I smoked a cigarette and waited. She finally arrived at ten of seven.

After she parked next to my Lincoln, she left her car and fell into my arms and hugged me tightly.

"I'm overjoyed he's been caught and scared right down to my toes at the same time," she said.

"Nothing is going to hurt you," I said. "I promise that."

"Driving over here my hands were shaking on the wheel," Ellen said.

"Let's go up to my place," I said. "Where's your bag?"

"Trunk."

*****

I relaxed Ellen by having us soak in a hot tub. The cats greeted her warmly and watched us from the bathroom floor.

Ellen placed a hot washcloth over her eyes and I filled her in on the day's events.

"He's really going to be there," she said.

"Us, too, but he won't see us," I said.

"I'm afraid I might lose it when I see him," Ellen said.

"You won't."

"I've been a recovering addict for ten years now and there isn't a day I don't wake up and have the initial urge to get high," Ellen said. "I go to work and go to meetings and take aerobic classes on my lunch hours and still it's always there, that urge to shoot dope into my veins. It won't take much to bring me to failure."

"That's not going to happen, not tomorrow," I said.

"I warned you not to become my addiction," Ellen said.

"You can lean on someone and gain strength and not become addicted," I said. "I leaned on my friend Davis for half my life. For friendship, protection, guidance and even advice. It has nothing to do with addiction, just human weakness."

"Were you shooting dope into your veins all that time?"

"No."

"Then you can't possibly understand my point of view."

"So what are you saying, what do you want to do?" I asked.

Ellen removed the washcloth from her face and looked at me. "Part of me wants to run as far away from you as possible," she said. "And part of me wants you inside me."

"Which part wants which?" I said.

Ellen stared at me for a second and then burst into laughter.

"I'm hungry," I said. "Eat in or take out."

"In."

"What would you like?"

"Chinese."

After we got out of the tub and toweled off, I used Ellen's cell phone to call the Chinese restaurant on Ninth Avenue and ordered half the menu. After I hung up, I said, "Forty-five minutes to an hour."

Ellen looked up at me with a smirk on her lips as she took hold of my sack. "Now what can we do for the next forty-five minutes?" she said.

*****

On her left side, Ellen hugged the cats while I hugged Ellen.

"What was she like?" she asked quietly.

"Who?"

"Your other woman, the one who left you for a woman, that's who."

"She was a cop."

"You already told me that and that tells me nothing."

"What do you want to know?"

"What did she look like, what did she like to do? Her personality. Things like that."

"She was tall, around five-foot-eight or nine," I said. "Dark hair and eyes and had a fierce temper. She was independent and hated to be taken care of. I think what drove a wedge between us was that while she was serving her time, I paid off her mortgage so she wouldn't lose her home."

"Did she offer to pay you back?"

"I did it without telling her."

"That was a mistake."

"I know."

"Did you suspect she was seeing a woman?"

"I did not."

"You're a complicated man, Kellerman."

"I'm not," I said. "That's why I didn't suspect."

"Yet you caught a man who evaded the FBI and police for ten years."

"Doing what I do isn't that difficult if you follow your instincts," I said. "If you suspect the brother did it nine times out of ten it turns out to be the brother did it. And like I said, I have an advantage over the police in that I don't have to follow their rules."

"Just your own?"

"That's right."

"I'm tired," Ellen said as she stroked the cats.

"Go to sleep."

"I'm also horny."

"Wait until morning. It will take the edge off," I said.

Chapter Thirty-one

We took a cab to the Federal Building in lower Manhattan.

Ellen wore a business suit of dark blue skirt that ended at the knee, a white blouse and matching blazer, no jewelry and little makeup. The three-inch heels brought her up to five-foot-four inches tall.

I wore a charcoal grey suit with a white shirt minus a tie.

We arrived at the Federal Building fifteen minutes early. Hawkins was waiting for us on the steps.

"Captain Larkin is already inside. Our names are on the guest list," Hawkins said. He looked at Ellen. She appeared pale and frightened. "It will be alright." He said.

"Go on up, we'll be along in a few minutes," I said.

Hawkins nodded and entered the lobby.

I dug out my pack and lit a cigarette.

"I'm ... sorry about this morning," Ellen said.

"Nothing to be sorry about," I said. "It's just nerves and completely understandable."

"I guess women can have performance anxiety as well as men," Ellen said, referring to the fact that earlier she was as dry as week-old toast.

I stepped on my cigarette and took her hand. "Let's go," I said.

Even though our names were on the list, we still needed to be screened before we were allowed entry past the lobby.

The interrogation rooms were on the sixth floor. Hawkins was waiting for us in the hallway.

"We are in here," Hawkins said and opened a door to a viewing room.

He opened the door and we entered. The interior was almost that of a comfortable living room designed to make witnesses feel relaxed and at home.

Cushy leather chairs faced a wide two-way mirror that overlooked the interrogation room.

Larkin and an FBI Agent were seated at a table.

A table had water and coffee.

Ellen and Hawkins took chairs. I filled a glass with water and gave it to Ellen. Then I poured two coffees and gave one to Hawkins.

The door opened behind us and a man around fifty entered.

"I'm Special Agent Doug Jones," he said. "The man with Police Captain Larkin is Special Agent Ford. He's about the best there is at conducting an interview."

"This is Ellen Fallen," Hawkins said. "I'm her attorney Cal Hawkins and this is my investigator Mr. Kellerman."

Jones looked at me. "I head about you from Captain Larkin," he said. "That was excellent work."

The door in the interrogation room opened and two agents led Brian Cosby in and to the table. Cosby's arms and legs were shackled.

Jones hit the switch on the speaker so we could hear.

"You can loop him to the table," Ford said.

One of the agents removed the shackles on Cosby's wrists and looped the right wrist to the iron ring mounted in the table.

I looked at Ellen. Her eyes were locked onto Cosby.

Wearing an orange jumpsuit, Cosby appeared thin as a rail as most junkies approaching forty often do. His long hair was falling out in clumps leaving open spaces in his scalp. His beard was nearly all grey.

"Comfortable?" Ford asked.

"As a chicken in a hen house," Cosby said. "Maybe you two clowns would care to tell me why I'm here."

"You know perfectly well why you are here," Ford said. "The arresting officers explained it to you when you were taken into custody after receiving your extortion money at the Walgreen's in Rhode Island."

"Where's my attorney?" Cosby said.

"Now why do you want an attorney?" Ford asked. "It will just complicate things and force us to remove our offer from the table."

"What offer?" Cosby asked.

"You're facing murder one for the murder of Mrs. Fallen, kidnapping of her grandson, conspiracy to sell the baby on the black market and blackmail and extortion," Ford said. "And that's just for an appetizer."

"That's not an offer, that's a laundry list," Cosby said.

"In exchange for information we will have you tried in Manhattan and not federal court," Ford said. "We will enter lesser charges against you and seek twenty-five years instead of life."

"What information?" Cosby asked.

"We want to know who Ross sold the baby to," Ford said.

I looked at Ellen. She was sitting forward in her chair with her eyes locked onto Cosby.

"Ask Ross," Cosby said.

"We did," Ford said. "He's in a hospital for people with Alzheimer's. Know what that is?"

"Ask his kid," Cosby said. "He was more than willing to pay to shut me up."

"To protect his name and family," Ford said. "He doesn't know anything about his father's criminal activities."

Cosby started to laugh.

"What's funny?" Larkin asked.

"Neither do I," Cosby said.

"You're saying you don't know who Ross sold the baby to?" Ford said.

"Why would I?" Cosby said. "This junkie pal of mine said he heard where we could score big if we could get our hands on a baby. That he knew this lawyer that dealt in the black market for stolen babies. As it happened, I knew where I could get my hands on a new born. Who knew that old bitch would put up such a fight?"

"Mrs. Fallen?" Ford said.

"Yeah, her. Who'd you think?"

"You murdered her and kidnapped the baby?" Ford said.

"Hey, he was my son," Cosby said. "Probably. My old lady was turning tricks, so who knows."

"Did you ever discuss with Mr. Ross where he was going to sell the baby?" Ford asked.

"No, and who cares," Cosby said. "I got paid fifty thousand for the kid. Ross could make cold cuts out of him for all I care."

I looked at Ellen. Her hands were by her side as she stared at Cosby.

"You don't seem to care very much what happens to you Mr. Cosby," Ford said.

"I've been a junkie for half my life," Cosby said. "A while back I contracted the AIDS virus. I was HIV positive for a while and now I have full blown AIDS. I'll be dead before you even get me to trial, do you think I give a fuck what you do to me now?"

Ellen gasped softly, but otherwise didn't move.

"Maybe so, but we can make what's left of your life very comfortable if you can tell us something, anything that might help us locate the baby," Ford said.

"Why not ask his bitch of a mother?" Cosby said. "If her mouth isn't full of cock that is. Cause I don't know shit."

*****

Hawkins and I waited in the hallway outside the ladies room while Ellen was in a stall vomiting up a case of nerves.

Larkin and Ford came out of an office and joined us.

"Murder one, kidnapping, selling a baby on the black market, blackmail and extortion," Larkin said. "We did good."

"Except for locating the boy," Hawkins said.

"We didn't really have much hope of that," Ford said.

"Well, we have a ton of paperwork to do," Larkin said.

Ellen was another ten minutes in the bathroom and when she finally came out, she was pale and shaking.

I placed my arm around her and we walked to an elevator.

"I'm sorry," Hawkins said. "I'm truly sorry."

*****

Back in my apartment, Ellen ripped off the suit and put on jeans and a sweatshirt.

"What are you doing?" I asked.

"Going out."

"Give me a minute to change," I said.

"Alone."

"Why?"

"I'm going to walk around Washington Square Park and find a dealer and get so fucking high none of this shit will matter."

"I can't let you do that," I said.

"You can't stop me."

"I can stop you."

Ellen reached into her handbag, came up with pepper mace and sprayed me right in the face.

The reaction was instantaneous. I dropped to the bedroom floor with excruciating pain in my eyes, throat, nose and skin.

Ellen walked out and I was powerless to do anything but roll around on the floor and wait for the pain to subside.

It took about forty-five minutes before I was able to stand up. I removed my clothes carefully to avoid contact with my eyes as a slight touch with clothing wet from the spray would start the process again.

I took a cool shower and washed my hair twice, then put drops in my eyes for the redness.

When I felt able, I tossed on a pair of jeans, tee-shirt and windbreaker to hide the .45 Browning, then went down the hall and told Mrs. Parker if I wasn't back tonight to check on the cats.

*****

I sat on Ellen's front steps with two containers of coffee and smoked while I waited. Hours passed and close to midnight, a yellow cab arrived and Ellen stumbled out and nearly slipped and fell.

She wobbled to her front door. I stood up and she looked at me.

"Kellerman?" she said as she fished for her keys in her handbag.

A moment later, she passed out in my arms.

*****

When I put her to bed I was grateful Ellen was just drunk and not high on drugs.

A drunk is easier to recover from than a heroin binge.

I removed all her clothes and placed several towels under her butt for that moment I knew would come.

When I was sure she wouldn't vomit and choke on it while asleep, I left her alone and went to the kitchen and made some coffee.

At the table, I drank some coffee and smoked and mulled things over for a while.

There was something I was missing, something right under my nose that I should be seeing but I wasn't.

Usually it the obvious that we miss. You get caught up in searching for evidence and clues and the *right under your nose* gets lost in the shuffle.

Brian Cosby was a useless pile of shit that should be put to death, but because of some very liberal laws would get life. If he was telling the truth about having AIDS, he probably wouldn't live long enough to stand trial. His own life had taken life from him.

Ross Sr. proved useless as well due to his Alzheimer's and the lack of records he kept of his illegal activities.

Ross Jr. was key to arresting Cosby, but until he was contacted by Cosby had no idea about his father's outside interests.

Around two in the morning I quit driving myself crazy and sprawled out on the sofa. I fell asleep almost instantly and didn't stir until after eight in the morning.

The first thing I did was check on Ellen. She didn't wake during the night and had urinated onto the towels as I figured she would. I didn't want to disturb her so I returned to the kitchen and made some fresh coffee.

Just before nine, when I was on the second cup of coffee and third cigarette, I heard Ellen stumble from the bed followed by sounds of vomiting.

I took my coffee to her bathroom where she was on her knees at the toilet. I sat on the rim of the tub while she puked it all up.

When there was nothing left, she flopped against the wall and looked at me.

"How did I get home?" she asked.

"Cab."

"Who put me to bed, you?"

"I did."

"Undressed me with the towels?"

"Also me."

"Good move," Ellen said. "I peed myself."

"Take a shower," I said. "I'll make you some breakfast."

"My stomach couldn't hold anything."

"It will," I said.

"Did I …?"

"You did," I said. "I'll be in the kitchen."

I returned to the kitchen, waited to hear the shower running and then took a mug of coffee to the backyard for a smoke.

When I returned to the kitchen, I dug around for a fry pan and started cooking eggs and some toast.

Wearing a robe and barefoot, her hair still wet, Ellen wandered into the kitchen and took a stool at the chef's island.

"My head is killing me," she said. "And my stomach can't hold any food right now."

"It will," I said.

"I guess I really blew it, huh?"

"Blew what?" I said as I flipped eggs.

"My sobriety, us, all of it in one sitting," Ellen said.

"You fell off the wagon after a very stressful event, don't beat yourself up over it," I said.

"I wasn't looking to get drunk," Ellen said. "I was looking to get as high as a kite on heroin."

"I know."

"When did they clean up the park? They were playing chess. There was a clown with balloons for God's sake."

"Ten years ago, maybe twelve," I said.

"Your face is burned."

"It's not a big deal."

"I maced you so I could run away and get high and it's not a big deal?"

"I survived and so did you."

"I peed in my own bed and you saw that," Ellen said. "And the puking and the drunkenness and …"

"Your eggs are ready," I said. "Eat. And the toast. It will settle your stomach."

Ellen looked at me.

"And water, lots and lots of water," I said.

*****

Ellen put her head back as I washed her hair.

"That feels so good," she said.

I massaged her scalp.

"And that's even better."

"Rinse and then I'm coming in," I said. "I could use a little cleaning up myself."

Ellen dunked under and when came up, I slid into the tub opposite her.

"Nothing rattles you, does it?" Ellen said.

"After you've been attacked by suicide bombing insurgent's hell bent on scattering your body parts to the wind, what back home is going to shake your cage?" I said.

"I'm damaged goods, Kellerman," Ellen said. "Are you sure you want to pal around with me?"

"Who isn't damaged goods?" I said. "Everybody I've ever met is fucked up in one capacity or another. Some hide it really well, others it right there for all to see it, but nobody escapes it all."

"Even you?"

"I live without a television, a phone and most of the basics that even those living in poverty have," I said. "My best friend is an imprisoned gay man who wants to kill me because he blames me for losing his boyfriend and my closest associate makes the Godfather seem like a choir boy, never mind the fact I have a raging hard-on for a drug addicted squirt who likes to mace me in the face when she isn't punching me. What do you think?"

"Is that your way of saying you love me?" Ellen asked.

"And don't make me repeat myself," I said.

"That raging hard-on you spoke of, could I see it?" Ellen said.

*****

We slept in the spare bedroom so Ellen's mattress could air out.

I was on my left side with Ellen's arm draped around my chest.

She was close to asleep when I rolled over and her eyes opened. I guided my left hand along Ellen's thighs until my finger found her opening.

"This is mine, yes?" I said.

"Yes."

"I don't share. Understand?"

"Yes."

"If I ever find another bull has visited the barn the situation will get ugly. Understand?"

"Yes."

There was a sleepy moment of silence.

"Can I go to sleep now?" Ellen asked.

"Yes," I said.

Chapter Thirty-two

I made breakfast while Ellen dressed for work.

She wore a black pants suit with three-inch heels and a white string of pears. She wore little makeup. She didn't need much.

I used her waffle maker and made a load of waffles with a side of bacon and coffee.

We ate at the chef's island.

"What you said last night about another bull in the barn, is that Kellerman's rule?" Ellen asked.

"It is," I said.

Ellen looked down at her plate.

"Does it apply both ways?" she asked.

"It does," I said. "Otherwise it doesn't work."

Ellen looked up and showed me a smile.

"I have to read a bunch of boring tax reports today, what are you going to do?"

"Find your son."

*****

I stared at the one hundred and thirty pound dumbbells on the rack at the heavy weight room in the Y. They don't get much use. I had done one set of ten reps of bench presses with dumbbells starting with the seventy pounders and worked my way up.

The bet with myself was ten reps with the one thirties after exhausting my chest beforehand.

I chalked my hands to keep my grip from slipping. Then I took hold of the one thirties and sat on the bench. After several deep breaths, I went prone with the dumbbells on my chest and started pumping out reps.

At eight I felt my chest start to go and rep nine went up at a crawl. I held the dumbbells above my head for a few moments and sucked wind. Then I lowered the dumbbells to my chest and pushed hard. At the midpoint I hit a wall and they wouldn't go, but I gave it all and completed the tenth rep and then let them fall to the thick rubber floor.

I stayed prone on the bench while I sucked in air and recovered. I half expected to hear Davis behind me talking shit, but I was alone.

Then I replaced the dumbbells on the rack and switched out the weight room for the track. I ran one hundred laps in thirty minutes and called it a day.

*****

"Check," Johnny said.

I studied the board. Then I slid my bishop in place to defend my king. If Johnny took the bishop, my knight was waiting to take his queen.

Johnny toyed with his mustache while he pondered his next move.

I lit a cigarette and waited.

Johnny moved a knight into attack position that, in three moves would corner my queen if I wasn't careful.

"So, have you given up the hunt for the boy?" Johnny asked. "The arrest has been on the news nonstop. Larkin will be polishing his new desk within a week so it appears."

"Somebody knows where the kid is," I said as I moved rook to block Johnny's bishop.

"Somebody?"

"Ross said it's impossible to hide even a single penny of income from the IRS," I said. "It stands to reason you can't hide a baby from …"

Johnny looked at me. "From what?"

"Can you get Ira down here?" I asked.

*****

Ira sat across the booth from us and sipped his drink of bourbon over ice.

Johnny had a shot of bourbon neat. I had a mug of coffee.

I lit a cigarette.

"I don't think you can smoke in here," Ira said.

"Never mind that," I said. "I have another job for you."

"I'm listening," Ira said.

"I was told it's impossible to hide a penny of income from the IRS," I said. "It stands to reason you can't hide a baby either."

"Hide?" Ira said.

"Birth records, school enrollments, things like that."

"Unless they're fake, which isn't all that hard to do."

"Even fake can be searched," I said.

"True. So what's the job?"

"Even if you hire an adoption attorney to help with the red tape and all the bullshit, you still need to go through Social Services if it's a legal adoption," I said.

"So?"

"So if you were to hack Social Services and check names of people waiting for babies and then some names disappeared from the list without having adopted, maybe somebody bought a baby on the black market," I said. "And then if you checked those names for birth records of babies and found a forged birth certificate and hospital record, then maybe we have what we're looking for."

Ira stared at me.

Johnny stared at me.

"Cool," Ira said.

"Twenty grand sound alright?"

"I'll be back tomorrow around this same time," Ira said.

"Cool," I said.

After Ira left, Johnny said, "How about another game?"

*****

"As soon as you get off work tomorrow, drive straight to the Pub," I said. "I'll be waiting for you there."

"Suddenly I feel frightened," Ellen said.

"Don't be," I said.

Ellen sighed.

"Is it against Kellerman's rule to say I love you?" she asked.

"Nope."

"I love you and seemingly more each day," Ellen said.

"And he said?"

"I'll say it just once and that should suffice," I said. "I love you too."

"Good," Ellen said.

After I hung up, I returned the phone to Mrs. Parker and went to my apartment.

Ellen's open suitcase was still on the bedroom floor where she had left it and both cats had crawled into it and were sound asleep.

I guess the cats didn't know about Kellerman's rule and if they did, they certainly didn't care.

Chapter Thirty-three

In the morning I went to my bank and deposited the cashier's check for fifty thousand into my account and then visited my safe deposit box located in the basement vault.

The box contains two hundred thousand in emergency cash. I took twenty thousand with me.

At home, I changed into sweats and headed down to Roth's gym. I gave it a little extra on the heavy bag after jumping rope and working the speed bag.

Afterward I sat with Roth and watched a pair of promising middleweights spar four rounds.

"Today happens to be my birthday," Roth said.

"I didn't know that," I said. "How old?"

"Eighty-two."

"Well, happy birthday," I said.

"Yeah, fuck it," Roth said.

*****

A letter from Davis waited for me in the mailbox when I returned home. It contained his next move in our game.

I took a quick nap, and then shaved, showered and dressed casually in jeans, pullover shirt and walking shoes. I tucked a thick envelope with the cash into the small of my back and covered it with my shirt.

When I entered the Pub, Johnny was at the bar and I sat at an empty stool.

Johnny set me up with a mug of coffee and a shot of bourbon for himself.

I lit a cigarette and took a few sips of coffee.

Two stools to my right, a man drinking boiler makers looked at me.

"Hey, pal, no smoking in here. City law," he said.

I ignored him.

"Did you hear what I said?" the man said.

"Is there a problem?" Johnny asked him.

"Well, obviously. That man is smoking."

"So he is," Johnny said. "Do you wish to make a complaint?"

"Yes," the man said.

"Do you see the fat man drinking tequila with two women at the table in the corner? The man smoking a cigar. He is from the Board of Health. Make your complaint to him," Johnny said.

"What kind of a bar is this?" the man said.

"The kind where people can enjoy themselves," Johnny said. "And mind their own business. Now I'll ask you to choose. Behind door number one my friend will take you out back and beat your brains in. Behind door number two your drinks are on the house."

The man looked at me and then slowly faced front.

"We have a winner," Johnny said.

In the mirror, I saw Ira walk in. He approached the bar and sat next to me.

"Ellen isn't here yet," I said.

Ira nodded. "I'll take a bourbon," he said to Johnny.

I looked at my watch, then left the bar and went to the parking lot. Ellen was actually a few minutes early.

"I left work and drove straight here," she said as she hugged me.

"Ira's waiting," I said. "Come on."

*****

Ira sat behind Johnny's desk. Ellen and I took the chairs while Johnny leaned against his file cabinet with a glass of bourbon.

"This Ross was a genius," Ira began. "He knew it's easier and safer to create a new baby than a new identity. For a new identity you need birth certificates, social security numbers, school records, job records, tax records and a bunch of other shit. But for a baby, all you need is a birth certificate and hospital records."

"You mean fake ones?" Ellen said.

"That's what I mean," Ira said.

"And?"

"Jeeze, can't a guy build some momentum to the story?" Ira said.

"Ira, we need …" I said.

"Warlord Emperor," Ira said. "Or just Warlord will do. This is, after all, an official visit."

"The warlord is about to have his ears pinned back," I said.

"Okay, okay," Ira said. "He removed a folded sheet of paper from his jacket and opened it. "I did as you asked and hacked into Social Services and …"

"You hacked Social Services?" Ellen said.

"Hey, it's how it's done," Ira said. "I could call them up and ask, but they're kind of stingy with their information."

Johnny tossed back his drink and said, "Ira. I mean Warlord; do you see that purple vein on the side of Kellerman's neck?"

"I see it," Ira said.

Ellen turned and looked at my neck.

"Usually, what it means if you see that purple vein is that you will never see anything again," Johnny said. "I strongly suggest you get on with your report and as quickly as possible."

Ira looked at me. "Where was I?"

"Hacked Social Services," Johnny said.

"Yes, thank you," Ira said. "As Kellerman suggested, I hacked into SS and checked ten years ago who was on the waiting list for adoptions. Then I went back five years prior to that to see who was waiting for a number of years and I found this couple from New Jersey. Six years on the list."

"Why so long?" I asked.

"They wanted a new born to less than a year old so they could raise it as their own," Ira said.

"And?" I asked.

"Ten years ago their names vanished from the list."

"Because?" I said.

"Well, they didn't adopt, that's for sure," Ira said. "No papers filed, no nothing. They just pulled themselves off the list. They sold their farm and …"

"Farm?" I said.

"They owned a melon farm in western Jersey, do you believe that?" Ira said. "Watermelons, honeydew, cantaloupes, shit like that. Four hundred acres of melons. I never liked cantaloupes, but honeydew when it's ripe is delicious. So anyway, I probe deeper and what do I find but they have relocated to Ohio in the valley where they own a new farm and also grow melons. Only this time they have a son. A newborn son. He has a birth certificate and hospital records and both are fake. Good quality that would stand up to ordinary scrutiny but not to a pro like myself. Helping this couple with the red tape and bullshit at SS is none other than the attorney they hired, one Michael Ross Senior."

"What are their names, the farmers?" I asked.

"Horace and Martha Plummer," Ira said.

I looked at Ira.

"I know, right," Ira said. "Who names somebody Horace?"

"Horace's parents," I said. "Background on them?"

"He's forty-eight, she's forty-seven and she had ovarian cancer and had them removed," Ira said. "Hence the need to adopt."

"Hence," I said.

"They're also a couple of Bible beaters if that means anything," Ira said. "Oh, I managed to snare a few pics from the boy's school. Check it out."

Ira removed a few three by five photos from the envelope and passed them to me. I looked at them and gave them to Ellen.

"My God he looks just like me," Ellen said.

"Contact information?" I said.

"It's all in here," Ira said and handed me his report.

I dug out the twenty thousand and set it on the desk. From my pocket I took out the last of Ellen's expense money and set it on the envelope. "Three thousand bonus money, okay?" I said.

"Who am I to argue?" Ira said.

"Come, Warlord, allow me to buy you a drink at the bar," Johnny said.

Johnny and Ira left the office.

I sat with Ellen.

She was looking at the photos. "This is really my son," she said.

I took the photos and tucked them into my pocket.

"Let's go," I said.

*****

Ellen sat in my tub with her hands over her knees and nervously rocked back and forth. "My son is a beautiful boy," she said.

I stripped down and got into the tub opposite her.

"I want him," Ellen said. "He was stolen from me and I want him back."

I reached over the rim of the tub for my cigarettes and lit one.

"I gave birth to him," Ellen said. "I gave him life, he's mine."

I blew a smoke ring and watched it float up to the ceiling.

"Technically those people are criminals," Ellen said. "They bought my son on the black market and that makes them criminals."

I blew another smoke ring and watched it rise and fade.

"Criminals don't deserve my son," Ellen said. "We'll go there and explain the situation to them and bring my son back. He's still entitled to his inheritance, but he's also entitled to know who his mother is too. And I'm his mother, not some criminal who purchased him like a slave at market."

I touched the cigarette to the water and then tossed the butt into the toilet.

"You'll help me. We'll go together," Ellen said.

"That wasn't our agreement," I said.

"They are criminals, Kellerman. Partly responsible for the murder of my mother," Ellen said.

"That wasn't our agreement," I said.

"Do you want my son growing up raised by kidnappers and murderers?" Ellen said.

"That wasn't our agreement," I said.

Ellen lunged forward and slapped me across the face.

"Stop saying that," she yelled.

I looked at her.

"I'll go alone," she said. "I don't need you. Your services are no longer required."

Ellen stood up and stepped over the rim of the tub and ran into the bedroom.

I stood up and got out of the tub and toweled dry. In the bedroom, Ellen was curled up on the bed, sobbing into a pillow. I laid down beside her and she turned and looked at me.

"It's not fair, Kellerman, it's just not fair," she said.

"No it isn't," I said. "But you'll live with it."

Ellen moved closer and snuggled her face into my chest. Her hair was still wet and I stroked it lightly.

"I ... can't be trusted right now," she said.

"I know."

"You need to help me."

"I will."

"I'm a great deal of trouble aren't I?"

"We'll meet with Hawkins tomorrow to arrange the boy's inheritance and then I speak with Mr. Cosby and hold him to his pledge to match the funds," I said. "Then I'll fly out to Ohio and see the Plummer's."

"And while you're gone I could crack again," Ellen said. "I'll go with you."

"If you saw the boy what then? It would make it worse. I have a better idea."

"What?"

"Can you take time off from work?" I said.

Chapter Thirty-three

"I suppose we need to think of what's best for the boy at this point," Hawkins said. "The man who murdered Ellen's mother is behind bars, the attorney has Alzheimer's so there is no point going there and the boy is now ten and knows no other parents. I don't see the need to involve the police or FBI, do you?"

"No," I said.

Hawkins looked at Ellen.

"No," she said.

"And as Kellerman has been known to have somewhat less than a delicate touch at times, I shall accompany him to Ohio," Hawkins said. "Agreed?"

"Agreed," I said.

"I shall contact Mr. Cosby and arrange for his pledge," Hawkins said. "We'll fly to Ohio tomorrow."

I looked at Ellen and she nodded.

"Agreed," I said.

*****

Cindy watched Ellen carefully from where she stood beside Johnny's desk. Johnny sat behind it while Ellen and I took the chairs.

"I need help," Ellen said. "I'm a recovering drug addict and weak under pressure. While Kellerman is away in Ohio, the pressure of ... losing my son a second time could cause me to crack. In short, I can't be trusted alone right now."

Johnny looked at Cindy.

"You want a baby sitter?" Cindy asked.

"If you will," Ellen said.

"How long?" Cindy asked.

"Starting tomorrow, three days," Ellen said.

"It's up to Johnny," Cindy said.

Johnny had a shot of bourbon and tossed it back before answering. "Cindy will stay with you while Kellerman is away," he said. "If you give her any shit, well just don't. The woman could fight in the UFC is she wanted. When she works her shifts, you will go with her. I'll put you to work in the kitchen washing dishes so you can't get into trouble. No pay, of course. Agreed?"

Ellen nodded. "Agreed."

*****

As we crossed the street to my apartment, Ellen took my arm.

"I need you to fuck me like there is no tomorrow," she said. "If, after your done I can still walk, you'll have to do it again."

"Agreed," I said.

*****

I packed for four days and left out the suit I would wear tomorrow. I locked all my guns in the wall safe in my bedroom closet and withdrew five thousand from the stash of twenty thousand I keep with the guns.

On the bed with the cats, Ellen watched me pack.

"Hey," she said. "I think I can still walk a little."

"That's because you insisted on being on top," I said as I went to the bed.

"Oh, no," Ellen said as I shooed away the cats and then parted her legs. "Kellerman, wait."

*****

Cindy dropped her suitcase in the living room and said, "I like what you've done with the place. Did it come with the cats or did you accessorize?"

"Better cats than mice," I said.

"Where's Sandra Dee?" Cindy asked.

The bedroom door opened and Ellen stepped into the living room wearing a robe.

"Better get going before I start to cry," Ellen said.

"See you in a few days," I said and picked up my luggage.

"How romantic," Cindy said.

As I reached for the door, Cindy said, "Where's the TV?"

*****

Hawkins picked me up curbside in his BMW and drove us to Kennedy Airport where we caught the noon flight to Columbus where we had a three hour drive to the lush farm lands along the Ohio River in the valley.

At the airport I picked up several newspapers and a paperback book. After takeoff, Hawkins opened his briefcase and turned on an electronic device.

"What is that?" I asked.

"A Kindle," Hawkins said.

I looked at him.

"You really are in the stone age, aren't you?" Hawkins said.

We landed on time at two in the afternoon and were in the rental car by two-thirty.

I drove and navigated by GPS.

We stopped once to make a pit stop and fuel up on coffee. Around five-thirty we were on a back country road is what is referred to by city snobs as the Heartlands.

The last several miles took us on a back road where we didn't see another car in either direction.

There was a turn off onto a dirt road to my right and the GPS guided us onto it where it ended at a large farmhouse. A hundred feet behind the house stood a large barn. To the right was a small corral with a few horses and a large tool shed.

An SUV wagon was parked out front.

I parked next to it.

We left the rental and before we could take the first step onto the porch, Martha Plummer came out from the house.

She was an imposing woman, tall with broad shoulders and long hair gone to graying.

"May I help you?" she asked.

"Martha Plummer?" Hawkins asked.

"Who are you?" she asked.

"Calvin Hawkins, attorney at law and this is Mr. Kellerman, my chief investigator," Hawkins said.

"Investigator? What's this about?" Martha asked.

"Your son," Hawkins said.

"You've come to take him, haven't you?"

"No my deal lady, we have not," Hawkins said. "We bring only good news for you and your family. May we come in and I will explain it all to you."

*****

After carefully explaining about the boy's inheritance, Hawkins gave Martha all the papers to read from Fallen's will and the matching pledge from Cosby.

"May I smoke on the porch?" I asked her.

"Yes."

I really need an excuse to walk back through the living room as I had inspected every square in of the large and spacious kitchen.

The living room was furnished in quaint is sturdy furniture. Dozens of photographs of the boy hung on the walls or were set on shelves and tables. A large crucifix hung on the wall behind the sofa.

A piano was cornered by the window.

I went out to the porch and smoked a cigarette. It was dusk and hard to see down the dirt road but by the kick up of dust, I knew someone was coming.

Probably Horace.

Earlier, Martha told us that the boy was away for the week at Boy Scout camp and wouldn't be home for three days.

Horace had driven to town to hire migrant workers as pickers for the harvest of melons, over three hundred acres of them, Martha said.

I finished the cigarette and returned to the kitchen where Martha had put out a plate of oatmeal cookies and a pot of coffee.

I snared a cookie.

"My husband will need to read all this," Martha said.

"Yes, of course," Hawkins said. "But believe me, it is all legal and your boy's to inherit."

Martha poured coffee and I ate another cookie.

The front door opened and Martha said, "That would be my husband."

Heavy footsteps came to the kitchen and Martha stood up.

"Horace, these men … what are you doing? Put that down," Martha said.

I turned in my chair as did Hawkins.

Horace was holding a .32 caliber revolver on us. He was a large, broad-shouldered man wearing a blue work shirt, overalls and heavy work boots.

"I always knew this day would come," Horace said. "Men would come to take our boy, our son."

"No, Horace, these men are here …" Martha said.

Horace cocked the .32. "You can't take what's ourin," he said.

"Mr. Plummer, I assure you that's not the case," Hawkins said. "The boy has …"

"We raised that boy from an infant to a young man," Horace said. "He's a God-fearing Christian and a fine boy."

"Horace, please read this letter," Martha said.

"Lies, Martha, all lies," Horace said.

"I assure you, Mr. Plummer, it's all true," Hawkins said. "Your son has …"

"That's right, he's ourin, not yours," Horace said.

I estimated ten feet separated me and Horace and from a seated position, if I rushed him, he had time to get off two shots. Two bullets from a .32 Magnum can do a lot of damage and even prove fatal.

"Martha, there's a roll of duct tape in the cabinet. Get it," Horace said.

Martha stood frozen behind the table.

"Are you deaf, woman?" Horace said. "Get the tape or I swear I'll put you in the ground with these two sinners."

Martha went to a cabinet and returned with a roll of duct tape.

"You, little man, turn your chair around so your back is to me," Horace said.

"Mr. Plummer, if you just listen to …" Hawkins said.

Plummer fired a bullet into the floor. Confined to the kitchen, the shot was deafening.

"Turn your chair around," Horace said.

Hawkins slowly stood, turned the chair and sat.

"Tape him good, Martha," Horace said. "I want to see his hands."

Martha went behind Hawkins and wrapped duct tape around his chest and arms until Hawkins was locked into the chair.

She stepped aside and Horace said, "Now the big one. Turn your chair around."

I stood, turned the chair and sat. I placed my hands by my side.

Martha stood behind me and began to wrap me in tape. She went around six times, ripped the tape and then stood back.

"Okay, Horace?" she said meekly.

"Go sit down and shut up, woman," Horace said.

Martha took a seat at the table facing me and Hawkins. She looked at me expressionless, but I could see the cry for help in her eyes.

Horace took a few steps forward.

"Nobody is taking our boy," he said. "He's a good Christian boy our son and he belongs here with us."

"We agree with you," Hawkins said.

"Shut up," Horace said. "You people spent a great deal of time and trouble to find us, do you really think I believe you want to leave here empty-handed?"

"If you'll just read …" Hawkins said.

"I told you to be quiet," Horace said as he took a few more steps forward.

Directly behind me I heard Horace sigh loudly.

"I'll allow you one minute to make your peace with God," he said.

The revolver touched the back of my head.

I put my left foot on the edge of the table and shoved backward while kicking upward with my right foot. I went over hard and the tip of my right shoe caught Horace in the face.

He stumbled backward as the back of my chair hit the hard wood floor. I yanked my arms forward to split the tape and freed them. I rolled out of the chair and jumped to my feet.

Horace had blood streaming down into his left eye from a cut on his forehead. He wiped it with his sleeve and looked at me.

Four feet separated us.

"Put the gun down Mr. Plummer," I said.

He did just the opposite and aimed the gun at me.

"Please put the gun down Mr. Plummer," I said.

He cocked the hammer.

I cupped my right hand and rushed forward and slammed him in the throat with my full weight behind the blow just as the gun fired.

The shot went wild and struck the wall.

His windpipe crushed, Horace sank to his knees and fired another shot into the floor. Then the gun slipped from his hand and he fell dead at my feet.

I turned and looked at Martha. A strange little smile was on her lips.

*****

"A meaner man never walked the earth," Martha said as we waited for the county sheriff and homicide detective from the state police to arrive.

We were in the living room having coffee.

"Boy Scouts, bible school, football, little league, nothing was good enough to satisfy Horace," Martha said. "If he got a B instead of an A, he got the buckle end of a belt. If he struck out in a game or didn't remember one of the Ten Commandments, he got the same. If I tried to interfere, I got the same, the buckle end of a belt."

Martha looked at me.

"Am I sorry he's dead?" she asked. "The answer is no."

"Do you mind if I smoke?" I asked.

"I don't mind," Martha said.

I lit up.

"I suppose I'll lose the boy after this," Martha said.

Hawkins looked at her. "Not if you let me do the talking," he said.

*****

"Let me see if I understand this," the sheriff said. "And feel free to correct me if I misspeak. You came here to tell the Plummer's that the biological mother of the boy has left him an inheritance and Mr. Plummer thought you came to take his adopted son away and in a fit of rage he tried to kill you. He taped you to chairs and was going to execute you but at the last second, Mr. Kellerman toppled the chair and broke free and managed to kill Mr. Plummer with a blow to the neck."

"That's about right," Hawkins said.

The sheriff looked at Martha.

"He's telling the truth," Martha said. "All of it."

"Does the boy know he's adopted?" the sheriff asked.

"We never told him," Martha said.

The homicide detective came into the living room from the kitchen.

"Two in the wall, two in the floor, broken chair and duct tape," he said. "It all checks out right down to the blood on Mr. Kellerman's shoe and the powder residue on Plummer's hand."

"What happens now?" Martha asked.

"In a month or so, Mr. Hawkins and Mr. Kellerman will have to verify their statements to the judge and then we close the file," the detective said.

"Do I have to tell him he's adopted?" Martha asked.

"Only if you want to," the sheriff said.

"Can I … can I tell him his father died of a heart attack?" Martha said.

"I don't see why not," the sheriff said and looked at the detective. "Do you?"

*****

Around midnight, we sat on the porch with cups of coffee. A bright moon illuminated the yard in front of the house. A soft westerly breeze gave some relief to the August heat.

"When we return in one month to appear in court, I will bring a check for the full amount of the boy's inheritance," Hawkins said.

"I suppose it won't harm my son none to learn that he had a long-lost aunt and she came to visit him when you come back," Martha said. "Would it?"

Hawkins looked at me.

"No, no, I don't think it would harm him at all," he said.

Chapter Thirty-four

Hawkins dropped me off in front of my building around three in the afternoon. Upon entering my apartment, the changes were immediately apparent.

On a new coffee table in front of the sofa sat a flat screen television. It was tuned to the cartoon channel and both cats were on the sofa watching the road runner foil the coyote.

Several scatter rugs adorned the otherwise bare floor.

A Bose radio occupied a new table against the wall.

Drapes hung from the windows.

The kitchen had several new appliances, including a new coffee maker.

There was a note taped to the refrigerator.

If I'm not here I'm across the street washing dishes. Sorry about the changes, but we were going stir crazy and needed something to do. I love you. E.

I changed quickly and went down to the Pub.

Johnny was behind the bar. Cindy was waiting tables.

I grabbed a stool.

"She's in the kitchen," Johnny said.

I nodded.

"How did it go?" Johnny asked.

"The boy's mother is a nice lady," I said.

"And the father?"

"Well, let's just say he's as cold as ice," I said.

"Want a coffee?"

"Later."

I left the stool and opened the door to the kitchen. The cook was at his station. Ellen was at the large sink, rinsing dishes to go into the dishwasher.

Her hair was up and frazzled. She wore a sleeveless blouse and shorts and was covered in sweat and scouring powder.

Then she spotted me and her entire face seemed to light up.

I walked to the sink.

"How would you like to be a long-lost aunt?" I said.

THE END